THE GENESIS CHAIR

by

William "Skip" Simonds

Cover art by:

Arseniy Korablev,
3D Artist, Animator, Programmer
Creator of Teya Conceptor
www.teyaconceptor.com
www.artstation.com/artist/arsdraw

To Victor Appleton
and
Victor Appleton II

I know both of you are not real and are just pseudonyms for many different men and women, but to a 10 year old you were the greatest writers ever. Thank you, you unknown and unappreciated authors. You gave this 10 year old a love of science fiction that survives to this day.

Acknowledgements

The creation of this book was in almost all ways a joint affair. Only people who have never written anything to be published think that authors are the be all and end all of the finished product. The truth is that it takes a community.

First in line for thanks, is my wife, Betsey deGroff. She hates science fiction but she loves me, so she struggled through the early drafts to provide valuable insight and even more valuable moral support. Thank you, sweetheart, for giving up your time with me on those late evenings when the story was flowing and those quiet afternoons when you let go of too many things so I could write. I love you. You are the best.

There are a whole host of others I need to thank who offered to read and comment on this work. Thanks to Sadie Clare, Kate Bedell, David Wylie, Hart Townsend, and Raphael Goldhirsch who without any particular love of the genre waded through all or some of the manuscript. Your willingness was encouraging and your insights were truly valuable.

Special thanks goes to a good friend I've never met: Andrew Faraday, who sight unseen offered to help with editing tone and content. Andrew is a true sci-fi buff and his commentary has been critical to shaping this into a decent work.

Next is another good friend I've never met, Arseniy Korablev. Arseniy is a gifted artist and illustrator whose art I discovered as I was looking for ideas as to what my Genesis Chair would look like. I found exactly what I was looking for. In fact, it was as though the artist had rendered the chair directly out of my imagination, complete with an abandoned town as the backdrop. I reached out to Arseniy directly, introduced myself, told him what I wanted to use the picture for, and offered to pay a license fee. Arseniy would hear none of it and graciously donated his artwork for free. The cover is amazing and it is all due to him. If you like his work (and he has more) please reach out to him directly. Thank you, Arseniy. Your generosity will not go unrewarded.

But far and away, the person to whom I owe the greatest thanks is Stephanie Lugg. Stephanie is a friend of more years than I want to admit who is a brilliant research lawyer in her own right, who has read every single word in this book at least twice, and many, more times than that. Her editing skills are unrivaled and for that alone, I am in her debt. But her questions about murky passages, noticing of whenever there was a lack of continuity, and her total non-sci-fi approach (she's not a fan which makes her input even more valuable somehow) actually shaped much of what this book is. And she did all of that while fighting her own significant health battle. Thank you, Stephanie. You rock!

Table of Contents

"To judge a man merely by success is an abhorrent wrong; and if the people at large…grow to condone wickedness because the wicked man triumphs…by such admiration of evil they prove themselves unfit for liberty."

– Theodore Roosevelt

CHAPTER 1 - **First Contact**

Dear Reader,

I do not expect you to believe what I am about to lay before you. I am not sure I totally believe it either, but I am compelled to pass it on to you, at least for your consideration. Do with it what you will. Only I beg you not to set it aside, lightly or otherwise. Consider it. Please.

It started with a chance meeting in a small bakery at Victoria Station. I was there to meet a colleague and had arrived, as usual, way too early. I am very impatient with those who are late for meetings with me, and so am very impatient with myself when meeting others. That day I hit every conceivable "green light" and was at the arranged spot a full hour ahead of time.

A nondescript gentleman asked if a seat at the table I occupied was taken, it being the tail end of rush hour and there being no other place to sit. As it was taken, but not for another hour, I told him he was welcome to sit with me.

His name was Sandborn. And he was, if he was to be believed, a time traveler.

And he was specifically looking for me. Or so he said. I asked him how that could possibly be as this Sandborn was totally unfamiliar to me by name, feature, or manner. He assured me we had never met before, but that he was well aware of who I was, and that he specifically had sought me out.

When I asked why, his answer was, to put it mildly, unsettling. He told me about a book I had written many years ago when I was an active minister which had come to his attention...in the year 2345. He added the year almost as an afterthought, a mere detail that might as easily have been left out as irrelevant or unimportant.

Now, dear reader, don't mistake this retelling of the meeting as an accurate recounting of the unfolding of all this. My intent is merely to make you aware of how this affair started...the bones of it, as it were. In truth, he did not sit down and say, "My name is Sandborn. I'm a time traveler from the year 2345, and I've come to see you here and now because of a book you've written and another one you are going to write." Had he done that I would have politely got up from the table, excused myself, and left without hesitation. One comes across all sorts in the Tube and some are more benign than others. I avoid "the others".

No. In truth, he was an intelligent, seemingly rational man, who engaged me in a conversation about the common problems of being a commuter in London...the kind of thing one talks about with strangers on public transit. I told him I was there to meet someone about business. He told me he was doing the same. He had an idea for a book, and he was going to meet an author to discuss writing it.

I am an author, although not a particularly well-known one. My books are not generally for the larger public, but primarily to support my public speaking career. I had written a book on men's personal development, an area of particular interest to me. It never sold well at all, and almost never outside of my seminars.

Nevertheless, I am an author, and even not particularly well read authors like myself are proud of whatever literary accomplishments we have, however small. When I told him I was an author, he told me he knew; that he had recognized me. I was mildly pleased that he was one of the very few that had read anything I had written, and that he was familiar enough with it to recall it, and me.

And then he told me the thing that changed everything. He told me I was the author he was here to meet, and that he was going to tell me a story that I would turn into a book, and that this as yet unwritten book would change the future.

I had no reason to believe him. But he spoke from such a place of confidence, such a place of assurance, with such surety I was transfixed. He was either insane, a con man, or someone who sincerely believed he was telling me the truth.

Whichever, this chance meeting had captured me. Maybe there was a book, or at least a good short story in it, but I would never know if I walked.

It was a crowded and very public place. He was roughly my age and had no weapon that I could discern. There was a police presence. I felt reasonably safe for the moment. I decided to challenge him.

"How can you possibly know that? You are just selling an idea."

"No, sir. Mr. Simonds, I've read your book on the mature man and it is good, very good, but it has never sold very well. In fact, you have to access the Library of Congress to find a digital copy. You see, I'm not from around here and where I'm from, well, your book just isn't a thing."

"Well," I said, "of course my book isn't a big seller and wherever you're from, it wouldn't be a big seller. It isn't a big seller here or in America where I wrote it. So of course you couldn't find it in print. But it is available on Amazon, and unless you are from some back corner of the Amazon River, you could order it online and have a printed copy by post."

I continued. "But there is a flaw in your tale. I have only just submitted it to the Library of Congress and I was told it would take 6 months or more for it to be digitized. They no longer keep hard copies. You couldn't have possibly gotten a copy from that source."

"You are right, of course," Sandborn said, "for 2020. But I wasn't speaking of this year."

He paused, put both hands gently on the table, palms down, took a deep breath, and looked up and directly into my eyes.

"I am from 2345. I am, whether or not you accept it, a time traveler. I have come back to this year, this day, to meet you. Not because of the book you have already written, but because of the book you are going to write for me. If you write it, I believe it will change the future course of events for humankind."

"I don't believe you."

"You shouldn't, at least as far as this conversation has gone. But let me help you. You are here to meet Arthur Wellington, an official with the Anglican Church. He has asked to meet you to discuss holding a series of seminars here in England. You've never met him face to face, but he will identify himself by carrying a copy of your book, The Measure of a Man; something both he and you are totally convinced would not happen by accident, given how little the circulation is. He will not show up, unfortunately. He will call you later to apologize. He will tell you he tried to reach you earlier, but he could not get you to answer. When you leave the Tube after waiting, your phone will update with his attempts as you do not have reception here. In the meantime, as you wait, you are going to work on a manuscript you're writing as a sequel to The Measure of a Man. That manuscript, which you have not talked to anyone about, even your wife, which in fact you just started on the plane last night, is part of what I want to talk with you about."

"How could you possibly know about this...any of this?" I was dumbfounded.

"I have not followed you or spied on you. As I said, I have never met you before...at least not before now, nor have I met anyone who knows you. I have not hired a private detective or used any digital means to stalk or investigate you.

"There was no need to do any of that. I know all of this because you will write about this meeting in the opening chapter of another book I'm going to get you to write in addition to the one you started last night on the plane, and the opening chapter in this one will be a letter to the reader describing this meeting. I have seen and read its opening section."

"But..." I stammered, "that's impossible. How could you read what I haven't written?"

"Well, I knew you would probably think I was crazy or a con man, so as someone who can travel through time, I made a stop a few weeks in the future, sort of "on my way" to meet you here. You were very glad to see me, and we discussed and I helped you write the opening section of your manuscript. That's the funny thing about time travel: stuff doesn't have to happen linearly. I said a moment ago that I had not met you before, as in before now, this moment, something behind you in time. I was telling the truth. I have not met you before now in this timeline. But I did meet you for the first time in my timeline on my way here from the future. It was funny in a way. For you, it was the second time. I was familiar to you. That you were happy to see me told me this meeting ended well. And you willingly told me all the details I needed to know to convince you. You even told me the time and place to meet you."

Dear Reader, at this point all this seemed to me to be just so much suggestion. He could say everything he was saying and just be making it up. I had made no secret of my meeting with Wellington or the purpose for it. I assume Wellington had not either. Perhaps I would write a book about a time traveler, perhaps it would have a "Dear Reader" opening chapter; but that could all happen simply by the power of his present suggestion. It would be no more than a self-fulfilling prophecy. There simply was no proof other than the possibility of the missed calls from Wellington...but that, too, could be explained as a shrewd guess based on some circumstance in Wellington's day that Sandborn could have engineered.

"Now look here, Sandborn. You are expecting me to believe all of this without the slightest shred of evidence supporting what you are saying. Your future visit to me as you describe it could be nothing more than a figment of your imagination. I'm to believe that you are from the future, have a time machine, want me to write a best-selling book, and you expect me to believe that such a book will change the future of the world. Rubbish. It is all so stilted and has been done before. Soon you'll suggest that I need to 'prime the pump' or put 'some skin in the game' by investing some capital in the project. I can see the future too, and that is what I see coming.

"The simplest explanation suggests you are, in fact, a confidence man...Occam's Razor and all that. I am not buying into this in the least." I was gaining confidence now in my skepticism.

Sandborn seemed not the least bit bothered by my tirade. In fact, he looked like he expected it. But then that would be the talent of a good grifter: use the mark's reaction to your own advantage. Disarm him by agreeing with him. Appeal to his ego and, if possible, his greed. And Sandborn did not disappoint.

"You are right, of course. How could I disagree with you? What could I possibly say to convince you of the truth of what I'm saying? There is literally nothing."

But then he reached inside his coat pocket and handed me a folded up piece of paper. I opened it. It was dated two weeks hence. It simply said, "Believe him" and it was in my handwriting and signed by me.

Below, there was a post-script. "You're thinking this note is a forgery. Ask him to relate the dream to you."

I looked up at him, still not entirely convinced. It was clearly a forgery. I had not written it. But "the dream"? I have had many memorable dreams over my lifetime. In fact, I've used them as illustrations in my books and from the lectern. If I had written this note, though I was sure at this point that I hadn't, but if I had, there was only one dream I would be referring to.

"Well?" I said.

"It is the earliest, first dream that you remember having. You dreamed you were walking along a small cul-de-sac with a row of houses exactly the same. The big city was in the background in the distance. On the right-hand side of the street, a little girl your age sat on the front steps of one of the houses. You walked up the sidewalk towards her and no word was ever spoken, but you fell in love with her in that instant...even at that tender age you knew what true love was. Then you awoke, and you never dreamed that dream ever again, but you have never forgotten it either. It is just as fresh today in your mind as it was the moment you awoke."

It was perfect. I had never told that dream to anyone, ever. Yet he knew it to the detail. Only I could have told it to him. Or had I told him or someone else about it before and just did not remember doing so?   It was possible, I suppose. However, it was unlikely that I would have failed to remember the telling of that dream to anyone.

Then he reached into his valise and drew out a Times dated two weeks in the future. It would take time…two weeks to be exact…but it would be impossible to manufacture a forged newspaper and have it be totally accurate down to the detail of every word in every story. In two weeks I would know.

Dear Reader, there is no point in going on.   Two weeks came and the morning edition of the Times exactly matched the copy I had kept safely tucked away for the past two weeks. I needed no further proof. And when he showed up at my hotel room later that morning, I dutifully wrote him the note he would need for the me of the past to read, related my dream to him in as complete a detail as I remembered it, and gave him my fresh copy of the Times to take with him.

In return, he spent the next two days relating the story I am about to tell you. As I said at the beginning: Do with it what you will.   Only I beg you not to set it aside, lightly or otherwise. Consider it. Please.

CHAPTER 2 - **The Story Begins**

No one really likes the long hauls.   A long haul is a life sucking monotony, especially with the unchanging scenery in the depths of space. The only people who think space travel is glorious are people who have never done it.

But the people who have; they know.   You don't enjoy it. You survive it.

In interstellar space on a long haul, there is just emptiness. And emptiness has weight. In fact, in interstellar space there is so much emptiness it has a soul-crushing weight. When there is no sun or moon, no day or night, no weekday or weekend, you are the only constant. You become the center of your universe. There are other crew members, but they are just so many satellites in orbit around you. They don't matter except as they relate to and affect you.

Surviving long hauls isn't easy. Without a plan, long hauls may not kill you all at once, but they definitely eat away at you with each trip. Most guys aren't smart enough to know that.   Most guys don't have a clue and don't have a plan. They die a little every trip and they don't even know it.

I saw early on what happens to the crew and I decided it wasn't going to happen to me. I have a clue and a plan. I survive by having a bit of routine.

Even when the only thing to live for is yourself, there is still a need for routine. I'd seen crew go crazy for a lack of routine.

Some couldn't find the motivation to get out of a bunk and would sink daily, deeper and deeper into an abyss of lazy, self absorption. They'd end up more or less living cadavers of no or the absolute minimum activity. Some called them the walking dead.

Others would never get in a bunk unless they were passed out. Self absorption took them to heights of a kind of permissiveness that ultimately led to a non-stop gratification.

Me? I'm somewhere in the middle. I use routine to ground myself. I see the errors of the extremes and I have no desire for that kind of self consumption. Oh, I'm as self-centered as the next guy, but you've got to have some sort of internal system of discipline versus reward to actually enjoy the rewards.

My name is Deke Sandborn. I am the executive officer on the CS Rapacious, a cargo ship for hire operating generally within the solar system. Most of our runs are within the zone bounded by Venus and Saturn, but we'd take the occasional contract and make the not infrequent long haul outside the solar system, up to 500 parsecs.

"You got everything you need, Mr. Sandborn?"

"I do, Angie. Tell the watch officer I'll be there shortly. And how many times have I told you, call me Deke."

"Yes, Mr. Sandborn"

I knew that was never going to happen. Angie was a small man, both in size and thinking. He had his niche and it was there his thinking and behavior stayed. I liked him...as well as I liked anyone, which is to say not a lot. On a cargo ship you don't think about that kind of stuff. Angie was Angie. He was what he was and was never going to be anything else.

Angelino Ariti, steward to Captain Ahriman and myself, never seemed to sleep. He was always there to make sure I was up and out of the rack to stand my watches, attend Captain's Mast when held, got hot meals, and that my laundry got done and other housekeeping details.

Being a steward is a crap job, but everyone started there and worked up, unless like me, you graduated from a Maritime Academy[1] and came aboard as a rookie officer. Angie started at the bottom and just never went up. That never happened. Usually guys hated that post. But then, they were supposed to. That's the way the system worked.

Competition is what caused a cargo ship to work, and base servitude was designed to be despicable and demeaning to create a craving for advancement. And that craving was the birthplace of ambition which inevitably led to direct

---

[1] Forgive me for inserting myself in Sandborn's story. There are just things that Sandborn had to explain to me to make his story make sense. I think you may have some of the same questions I did, so perhaps by the judicious use of footnotes, I can explain somethings without interrupting the story. This reference to Maritime Academies is a good example. My assumption (and perhaps yours) had always been that space travel would have come about as a result of efforts made by the military. Thus, shipboard organization would have mirrored military organization. According to Sandborn, there are military vessels in space, but they are few and far between. The bulk of space vessels are commercial and grew out of our maritime tradition. Apparently the cost of space travel quickly outstripped the ability of governmental agencies to fund it and almost as soon as it was possible, prolonged space travel became the province of commercial enterprises. Our maritime academies that trained earthly seafarers quickly transformed themselves and became a primary source of qualified spacefaring crew, at least in the officer corp.

competition with anyone and everyone else. You weren't recognized and promoted. You clawed your way out and up.

It wasn't any different for officers. We just started on a little higher rung on the ladder.

Angie had worked his way up from a "mess rat" to "first officers steward". Mess rats were at everyone's beck and call. They got all the dirty personal service jobs for the crew. They cooked, served, and cleaned up after meals. They did laundry. They were shipboard janitors of the crews personal spaces (think latrines).

From there, with a little ingenuity and hustle, a good mess rat ingratiated himself to a couple of key crew members who were in charge of various teams. They would become unofficial personal assistants to those guys. And when a spot on their team opened up, they'd fit that mess rat in.

Angie had a different career path. He just never stopped being a mess rat. But he got so good at it that he gradually worked his way up in personal service to waiting on "first officers". On the bigger cargo ships, first officers were the captain, the exec, and two or three department heads. On the Rapacious, it was just Captain Ahriman and me.

Angie was just fine with that arrangement. He had good quarters in officer country so that he could be near to us. Our food was his food (and a step or two better than the crew's). And while he was at our disposal at all times, there were only two of us. As a mess rat, even the best mess rats were still having to do whatever anyone in the crew wanted them to do.

The captain and I were not low maintenance by any stretch. We worked pretty much non-stop. Sleep was never a full 8 hours. It was always interrupted by watches, minor emergencies, and breaking up seemingly endless intra-crew squabbles.

For his part, Captain Ahriman pulled his weight. A lot of

captains rode their first officers and kicked back to an easier life. Not Ahriman. He was a cutthroat competitor and daily had to prove he was better than any man under his command. He was brutal, to be sure. Some guys couldn't take it and left as soon as a contract was over. He liked it that way.

The guys that stayed, like me, did it because we were smart enough to stay out of his way, let him be the big cheese, stroke his ego when necessary, and just not take his bullying personally. He was an equal opportunity bully. It didn't matter who you were. At some point during every contract, he was going to show himself bigger, better, stronger, nastier, or more competent than you. That's how he maintained his position on a spaceship where ultimately everyone wanted your job.

As I walked down passageways to get to the bridge, I went through my mental checklist for the watch I was assuming. On the larger ships, execs didn't stand watches. I didn't mind it because it kept me in touch with every aspect of the ship. A tightly run ship was a good ship...a ship that had a better than average chance of survival...a ship that didn't get lost...a ship that made a profit for its owners and its crew.

As I came on the bridge, the officer of the watch nodded to me. I was early. I was always early. And the officers who knew me thought that if they didn't engage me in small talk, I was likely to relieve them early rather than waiting until my watch began. So all I got was nods, which was just fine by me.

I responded to his nod with a crisp but quiet, "Officer of the watch, report!"

"Mr. Sandborn it is 23:45. As of 2300 every department reported in with operational parameters within limits. The only anomaly was engineering, sir, where Chief Miller reported he had the jump drives off line to effect an emergency repair in anticipation of our next jump. He expected the jump drive to be online before our jump at 00:30."

"What was the nature of the repair, Mr. Wilson?" The jump drive was the most essential system in our ship given the immense expanse of space. If they were to break down, we would be confined to sub-light speeds and getting from point A to point B might well take a lifetime or two.

"The chief said the temporal damper was off calibration by .001 millimeters. He wanted it dead on, Mr. Sandborn."

"One one thousandth of a millimeter? That's within tolerances, son. Why did Chief Miller not want to wait until we were back in port for this?"

It was puzzling. You don't want to mess with the lifeline of superluminal travel. If something wasn't "broke" you didn't fix it. Any misstep on the temporal dampers might cause the crew to age months if not years on each successive jump. The dampers worked hand in hand with the jump drive to negate the time issues with superluminal travel.

"Well, Mr. Sandborn, the chief acknowledged that. But he felt that having the crew age unnecessarily with every jump would be an unwanted aspect of this or any run. So he made the call. He probably should have asked for Captain Ahriman's or your permission first, but he made the call and did it. I understand his girlfriend back home is younger than he is, and well, he doesn't want to make that difference any greater than it already is."

"Mr. Wilson, you know as well as I do that tampering with the dampers in the middle of a long haul is risky. It's risky anytime we are away from port, but if we lost the ability to jump back home in our own system, it might cost us a couple of months of travel to get to a port. But on a long haul like this, losing jump capability means we die out here parsecs from anywhere. Mr. Wilson, you should have at least notified me if not the Captain about this before the chief did this. It should have been our call, not Millers."

"Yes, Mr. Sandborn. Won't happen again, sir."

I was mad and Wilson knew it, but I had to laugh. "Of course it will, Mr. Wilson. If I know Miller at all, I know he doesn't give a fig about what the Captain, you, or I think. On some level I admire that kind of self confidence, but on another I hate that about him. He's going to do what he's going to do when he's ready to do it. The only saving grace in any of this is that he is extremely good at what he does and nothing ever goes wrong. At least it hasn't yet, otherwise he'd have been booted off this ship ages ago."

I paused. Should I put Wilson on report for this breach of protocol? Procedure dictated I should. This was a serious matter and I was definitely going to have to tell the captain about it in my daily brief. But putting a permanent record in his file was probably overkill. I didn't know for sure, but was pretty confident that, knowing Miller, Wilson found out about what Miller was doing only after Miller took the dampers off line. There would have been precious little anyone could have done at that point, so I decided to let it go. Besides I wouldn't want to be in Wilson's or Miller's shoes when Ahriman was on the warpath. That was probably enough of a correction for now.

"Very well then, Mr. Wilson. I'll inform the captain later. I have the watch. You are relieved at..." I glanced at the bulkhead clock..."23:55."[2]

---

[2] Sandborn explained the principle behind the jump drive to me. He said it would be necessary to the credibility of the story. Apparently deep within the bowels of the Rapacious was a matter/antimatter breeder. The breeder feeds the equivalent masses of matter and antimatter to the jump drive which combines them, suddenly, outside the craft. Normally this would be the equivalent of the biggest atomic bomb ever exploded times some huge number. But

because of the way the matter and antimatter were shaped, the energy is taken by the jump drive and used like a massive black hole. In the formation, time and space are bent. Like a sheet that a heavy ball is dropped on, the edges of time and space fold in until what was remote actually touches for a micro-millisecond and then, as the energy dissipates, slowly at first, and then faster than light, space and time snap back to their original shape. However, while space and time are bent and the far edges virtually touch, the Rapacious simply moves across the bridge to the far side. Positioned on the far side of the depression, as time and space re-expands, the Rapacious is pushed like a surfboard on a wave until the energy is dissipated. In this way the ship moves lightyears in milliseconds. So "faster than light" travel is achieved, just not by speeding up the ship, but by bending space.

But such a process also bends time as well. Let's say the jump was 100 light years (which is a distance defined by a time - how far light travels in a year), then for a ship to go that distance, even at the speed of light, it would take 100 years. The crew would have died long before the destination was reached. When the jump drive bends space, it is also bending time. In reality, as the ship is positioning itself to "unfold" at a great distance, and actually goes that distance in milliseconds, the ship is also positioning itself in a future time, and so would experience traveling that time in milliseconds. So in a jump without something "dampening" the effect of time, just as the crew moved that distance in a millisecond, they would age 100 years in a millisecond. The crew would die of old age in that millisecond.

Even if the jump were shorter and within the expected life span of the crew, they would experience the time like sub-light travel, but all of it compressed within that millisecond. The human brain and body cannot process that. Psychologically it would cause a cascading failure of the brain's ability to locate itself in time and space...the result being mental and emotional catatonia; and physically, death by rapid aging if the jump was long enough to outlast a crew member's life span.

"Aye Aye sir. You have the watch. I am relieved at 23:55. I will note it in the log."

At that moment, every alarm on the ship's control panel went off.

"What's wrong?" Wilson cried.

"I don't know, Mr. Wilson. It sounds like every system in the ship is off line or malfunctioning. Get to engineering and report to me on the status of the matter/antimatter containment fields, on the double."

"Aye Aye, Mr. Sandborn!" Wilson's voice echoed from the passageway as he was already off the bridge and running back to engineering.

I'd have crossed my fingers that it wasn't related to the containment fields because if it was, that was a space ship's worst scenario. It was so catastrophic nothing else really mattered. But I didn't cross my fingers because I couldn't. I was too busy operating the control panel trying to figure out if we were all going to die.

However, and this is murky to me, by being a precise distance from the center of the matter/antimatter implosion, the effects of time are mitigated. The time damper is the element of the maneuvering and navigational systems that positions the ship in the precise necessary location. Note: I do remember back in the 1950's there were experiments with dynamite where even delicate objects would be preserved through an explosion if they were placed a precise distance from the point of the detonation. This must be that principle but on a huge and mind boggling scale.

CHAPTER 3 - **Confrontation**

"Wait! I think I've got an older star chart somewhere."
Wilson's fingers flew through the navigational computer's
controls. "Ah, here it is."

We needed a miracle. With the loss of the jump drive, we
were in deep trouble. At first it had seemed like providence
that we hadn't imploded into our own black hole with the
collapse of the matter/antimatter containment fields. If they
combined inside the ship, it would create an implosion to
turn us into our own black hole.

But we all breathed a sigh of relief when that didn't
happen. Later we learned Miller manually jettisoned the
antimatter to keep that from happening. That feeling of relief
was soon replaced by the growing realization that if we could
not find a place to put down, effect repairs, and regenerate
antimatter; we were doomed to die a slow death of either old
age or starvation, depending on when supplies ran out.
Without jump drives, we could only travel at sub-light
speeds. At best it would take decades to get back to
"civilized" space at that speed. We were still in the Milky

Way, but a hell of a long way from anything familiar.

Everyone's first assumption was that it was all Miller's fault that the containment system failed. But in fact, it wasn't. His work had nothing to do with it, but it was the fact that Miller was working on the dampers that saved us from instant reduction to a singularity. He literally was inches away from the main matter/antimatter control panel. Had he not been there doing the questionable repairs, we'd have flashed as a momentary mini-nova and then collapsed into something that swallowed up us, the ship, and most of nearby space. Seemingly without thinking he'd thrown the switch that ejected all the antimatter into space.

We were saved from instant death...but to what end? A slow and lonely one?

"What have you got, Wilson?" Captain Ahriman was his usual impatient self only worse by a factor of about a zillion.

"Captain, we're not in a sector of space that is well mapped. Most of the more modern charts only focused on more highly traveled areas. Where we are isn't even on the more up to date charts. In fact, there's not much detail of this sector even on older charts. But when I found out we were coming this way, I dug up some even earlier charts that are not as accurate overall, but provided more detail of our projected route." As Second Mate, Wilson had the responsibility for navigation, something he took so seriously we all considered him somewhat of a navigational nerd.

"Cut to the chase, Wilson." Ahriman was not happy with what Wilson was saying. It had been Ahriman's idea to cut a corner of space...a sort of short cut across the center of a more circular, longer, but more populated and well used route to get where we were going. It was a risk. It was a risk for just the reason that had happened to us. If anything went wrong, there was no help available. This predicament was Ahriman's responsibility...not because the containment fields failed, but because of the point is space where they failed.

"Well, sir, I think there is more in this sector than the newer maps show. Give me a second, sir. I think there might be some possibilities."

Tense seconds passed.

"There!" Wilson jabbed his finger at the holographic chart. "It's small and very dark, but it is solid and therefore should be locatable. We could be there in roughly a couple of weeks using our sub-light engines."

"There's no known system in this sector," I objected. "How old is that chart?"

Wilson rubbed his chin. "It is a pre-dynamic chart, so probably, what, 50 years old?"

"But if it is pre-dynamic, it is a static map. What makes you think it is still there? If there's no system in this sector then that has to be a rogue planet, and my old astral-nav course at the academy says those things don't hang around long. Some travel at 10% of light speed or more."

My hope was I was wrong and Wilson's chart was right, but my skepticism was saying the opposite. And as XO it was my job to be skeptical.

Pre-dynamic charts were next to useless in space. They were remnants of a time in space travel where we were confined to travel within our own solar system where positions and distances were all known. Static maps are like an old fashioned map on earth…a snapshot of things in a moment of time. That was fine for terrestrial earth where things don't move except over millennia, and then not very far. But in space, where things are VERY dynamic and move at incredible speeds over great distances, static charts were almost useless. You might target a planet in some distant solar system only to find when you arrived it was on the other side of that system. And that didn't take into account that the system itself was part of a galaxy that was itself rotating as well as moving through space.

So Wilson's small, dark planet which had no system to anchor it into a specific orbit was likely long gone.

But then, what other option did we have? There was nothing we could get to at sub-light speed in any of our lifetimes.

Apparently Ahriman came to the same conclusion as I did at the same time. "Does the chart give it a name?"

"Yes sir. ISD-6709-RP. But it is also designated 'Debris'. I'm not sure if that's a name or description. I guess the chart maker wasn't sure what it was."

Ahriman couldn't care less. "Set course for Debris...make maximum possible speed."

"Aye, Sir."

"Wilson, what's our ETA?" I knew his answer would be a crap shot.

"Well, Mr. Sandborn, if it is still where the chart says it is, and I have no idea what the likelihood of that is, 14 days."

Over the next 14 days, Ahriman was like a caged animal. He was brutish and confrontational with literally every member of the crew, including me. He was always competitive but this was to a whole new level. He wore his arrogance like a tunic. His insistence on being respected as captain bordered on the ancient kings' insistence on "divine right to rule."

He was captain, therefore he was infallible. He was captain, therefore he was to be obeyed instantly. He was captain, therefore his perspective invalidated all differing views. He was captain, therefore he was owed complete loyalty. All deviation was punishable.

Not that the crew behaved much differently. The walking dead pretty much stopped even walking. The egoists cultivated their own following of sycophants whenever Ahriman wasn't around. Pettiness reached new heights.

Suddenly every slight became an insult, every misspoken word a slander. Micro-fights broke out sporadically, seemingly without warning; and were over before anyone could react. A shove given, a punch thrown but none returned. Instead the recipient went to find someone lower in the pecking order to hurt.

It was as though when facing the end, men wanted to find and fix their place on the ship. To be abused by one but to abuse another was oddly and disturbingly satisfying, even reassuring. There was real anger, but also real fear masked by that anger. The anger gave rise to the abuse but the fear seized on the results.

Me? I was not unaffected. I carried a steadily burning anger in the pit of my stomach and a similar reservoir of fear in the back of my head. But rather than lashing out, I internalized. Suddenly everything in my life transformed into a routine. A little routine had kept me sane on other long hauls, perhaps a lot of routine would protect me from the fear of death.

I started doing everything with a slow deliberation. It was as though I had a manual of life in my brain and I was following the directions step by step making sure I did not skip a single one, even if they were totally unnecessary. My daily, no, minute by minute goal became to make no mistakes, to do everything perfectly.

Regimen and routine were my wingmen. Life suddenly became so much of a plodding step by step through a pool of molasses. I was consumed by method and execution. I did not think. I did not create. I only did.

Ahriman and I had our brushes over the period. He was micromanaging everything. And given that I had responsibilities second only to him, he was hovering over my shoulder more than anyone else aboard. But it all came to a head when I was in main engineering going over Miller's adjustments to the time dampers.

"Sandborn, what the frack are you doing now? You've been worse than useless for days now."

I didn't bother looking up from what I was doing, my back was to him. I'd had it with Ahriman. "Captain, I'm checking Miller's work on the time dampers. It will do no good to repair the jump drives if Miller screwed up the damping field. Jumping with malfunctioning dampers will kill us as surely as if we couldn't fix the jump drives at all. Go find someone else to ride."

"You're an idiot, Sandborn. We don't have jump capacity and we cannot repair jump drives outside of a port. And without jump capacity, we have no need of time dampers. You're wasting time. I need you riding Wilson, managing him, making sure he's on beam for Debris. I'm ordering you to the bridge."

"Come off it, Deegan." I was at a breaking point with Ahriman...captain or not. "You know as well as I do Wilson doesn't need supervision. This is bull. You're just giving orders for the sake of giving orders. He's a qualified watch officer and navigator. It is a waste of my time to look over his shoulder. And it's not my job to make you feel better. This recalibration is critical. I'm not leaving here until it is done. So, no Captain. Stuff your order. I'm staying right here and finishing what I'm doing."

"Why you...". I never saw Ahriman's move, but I felt it. His hand crashed down on my head. I don't know what he was holding but it hurt like hell. I could feel myself slipping out of consciousness, slipping toward a comforting blackness. Like the coward he was, he had hit me from behind.

The room was spinning, but my fury was more powerful than my loss of consciousness. Ahriman stood with his hands clenched at his sides, hovering over my bent torso. I was stunned. My instincts kicked in. There was no thinking or planning, only rage and the need to push him back and away from me.

Without warning, like a fighter emerging from a clench, I pushed myself erect. My arms pushed out, my back became a ramrod, and my head snapped erect as every muscle in my body either contracted or stretched to bring me upright. Such was my anger that my head hit the hovering Ahriman as the business end of a sledgehammer.

Instantly I saw stars and felt a numbing pain run down my spine to the soles of my feet. With my ears I heard the numbing crack of bone upon bone, the crown of my skull against the point of his chin. Then I heard the secondary crack of his teeth hitting teeth as his profanity-filled mouth slammed shut from the force of the blow.

I heard more than saw him thrown backwards and heard the sickening thud as his head slammed against the bulkhead. He slid slowly down into a sitting position against the wall. I remember thinking that except for the blood he looked like he was asleep. Darkness covered my own eyes and I fell, first to all fours, and then fully prone on the deck.

As I slipped into unconsciousness I knew what I'd done. I'd killed the Captain.

CHAPTER 4 - **Debris**

"Deke, I'm as sorry as I can be about this but you have to stay in your quarters."

Wilson wasn't sorry one bit. His wildest dream had come true. With the death of the captain at my hands, he'd leapfrogged over me and become acting captain. Oh, he had no love for Ahriman, but neither did he have any for me.

"Look Wilson, you need me. You've got a five star crisis on your hands and the lives of all the crew are in the balance. You need all the help you can get. You're not ready for this kind of responsibility. I am."

I was right and Wilson knew it. His time in service was barely a tenth of mine and he'd just been given the 2nd mate position with this run. Up to this point, he'd just been a green 3rd mate, which is more or less a glorified custodian, a little better than a training cadet, but not a lot.

Wilson responded by stiffening and reverting to my formal name. "Mr. Sandborn, what I know is that by code and custom when an officer is killed by another officer, especially in a case like this where a junior officer has killed a more senior officer, and that being the ship's master, you are to be confined and under custody until a full inquiry can be made. I'm playing this one by the book, sir."

I knew he was "playing it by the book" because in this instance, the book was in his favor. As acting captain while on a run, the "acting" part was superfluous. For all intents and purposes, Wilson was the captain. Period. If and when I was brought before a board of inquiry, if I was found innocent and returned to duty, he'd no longer be captain, I would.

And, ironically, it was the captain's responsibility to constitute and call a board of inquiry. It would be chaired by him, but the remaining two members would be the senior most crewmen aboard. Wilson did have a choice here. Since I was the senior most officer on board with Ahriman's death, and a board of inquiry is supposed to be made up of three members all senior to me as the accused, Wilson could take the position that no legal board of inquiry could be convened. In that case, I'd have a really long time to hone my solitaire skills.

Maritime decorum held that a junior officer could not render judgement on a senior officer. The reason for that was pretty straightforward. If that were possible, it would provide a legal cloak for mutiny. Drum up charges against senior officers, run them in front of a board of inquiry made up of the crew, and suddenly you have a legal ship takeover.

However, in this case, given the state of emergency at hand, Wilson had cause to waive that requirement. I wasn't the crew's favorite by any stretch, but I had to believe they'd feel they had a better chance of getting out of this mess with me at least helping instead of locked up.

"Deke, I don't have the crew to spare to stand watch by your quarters to insure your confinement. I expect you to remain confined on your own. You know what's at stake here."

He was playing the first name card here. I wasn't buying it.

"Are you going to call a board of inquiry?" I asked.

"No, Deke. I'm not. At least not until we get this crisis resolved. I can't spare the men or the time. If we find Debris, if we can land there, if the environment allows for external repairs, and if we can make them, then I'll consider it. And I know you're going to say I need your help, but I don't. At least not enough to have to put myself at risk that you might do to me what it looks like you did to the captain. I'm leaving you without a guard, but I'm putting the rest of the crew on notice that if they see you anywhere other than your quarters, they are to immediately notify me and escort you back to your quarters. And if I need to, I'll chain the door shut. I trust I will not need to."

"Aye, Captain." Brice Wilson maybe was green but he wasn't stupid. With no board of inquiry there was no way for the crew to know if I was the victim or the perpetrator with Ahriman. That meant they'd all be on the guard with me. And with no board there would be no one to challenge his authority. My only hope was that his head was in the noose right along with mine if we could not effect sufficient repairs. He didn't want to get to be a captain only to die lost in space anymore than I wanted to be a captive under any circumstances. If my help were critical, he'd ask for it. In the meantime he'd locked me in as surely as if he had chained the door.

In fact, the more I thought about it, even if he did need my help, he still wasn't likely to call a board of inquiry. He'd just press me into service. He had justification and precedence to keep me confined until we reached a port (if we reached a port) where a proper board could be convened. When you got a leg up on a senior officer, it was highly unlikely you were going to give that advantage away.

We were still a few days out from Debris when the news filtered down to me that it had been sighted. Well, this deep in space, sighted wasn't really the right term. It was visible if only as a growing black spot that blotted out the stars behind it. You couldn't see it except as a blank field in a heaven surrounded by stars.

As a courtesy, Wilson had allowed Angie to continue as my steward. After all, pending trial I was still the senior officer on board and having Angie wait on me, pass me news, and handle my needs kept Wilson from having to respond to me directly.

"Mr. Sandborn, Mr. Wilson says we should be in initial orbit around Debris in a little over 48 hours. Would you like me to see if he'd allow you on the bridge for a first glimpse?"

"Angie, I doubt Mr. Wilson has any desire to see me anywhere other than this bunk. But you can ask if you want to."

"Sir, may I have permission to speak freely?"

"Of course, Angie."

"Mr. Sandborn, you have won no popularity contests over the time you've been the First Mate on the Rapacious. But then no one does. Like almost all officers you are formal and aloof, although you are overly formal. You command from a distance. You're not part of any clique on the ship, and you don't make it possible for anyone to use you to get ahead. That makes you a little colder but otherwise no different from any other officer on this ship, all of whom are mistrusted by the crew.

"What you have done is what you haven't done. You haven't been a bully or a know it all. You haven't been someone filled with their own sense of importance. But most of all you haven't been unfair or capricious. And that puts you in some pretty rarified atmosphere among the crew.

"They don't like you particularly, but they do respect you. And it's funny in a way, they are not afraid of you either. I say funny because when the crew loses its fear of someone senior, that's like the scent of meat to a pack of hyenas. But in your case, they don't see you as a threat, so they don't feel the need to do you in. What I'm saying is that there has been some talk among the crew about you. Pretty much all the crew hated Ahriman and are well rid of him. There's half that don't care if you did it on purpose, because even if you did, their lives are better for it. The other half actually know you and just don't see you as being a murderer. Either way, the crew is feeling like Mr. Wilson is not treating you right.

"There's more on this ship than just Acting Captain Wilson. And Wilson knows it. He may not restore you to your old job, but he is feeling the pressure to give you the freedom of the ship. I'm just thinking that asking him to let you on the bridge for the initial orbiting sequence is a way to test and see if he is softening towards you."

"Jesus, Angie. And here I thought you were just a high class mess rat. You've got some gray matter going on up there." I tapped my forefinger on his brow. "I'm impressed. Proceed with your plan."

Angie smiled, turned, and left.

Two days later, Angie's plan came to fruition. The ship's intercom crackled to life.

"This is Acting Captain Wilson. Mr. Sandborn, report to the bridge. I repeat: Mr. Sandborn to the bridge."

It made sense he'd use the intercom. He'd want the crew to know what he was doing so I wouldn't get brained if someone thought I was somewhere I wasn't supposed to be. And it didn't hurt having the crew know that he was easing up on me a bit. Well played, Brice.

On my way I noticed that the crew averted their eyes as I passed them. It wasn't furtive or shameful. It was deliberate and intended to send a message. They didn't look down or away. They looked past me. I was seemingly invisible.

There was no saluting on a merchant ship so there was no convention that required they acknowledge or respond to my presence. But I knew this crew. I'd worked with some of them since my first run on the Rapacious. It didn't matter. To them I just was not there.

I got it. On any ship, where any shipmate might be an enemy or an ally, and that status might change without notice, you were wary to start with. The unspoken rules for relationship were inviolate. The first is that we don't have a relationship unless I know whose side you're on. The second is what have you done for me lately. The second meant every relationship had to be tested regularly and often as alliances shifted fast on a space ship. That led back to the first rule which is essentially that no relationship exists in uncertainty. You don't assume anything about anybody. And that was where the crew had me. Unless they knew my role and whether I was friend or foe, I might as well not exist.

Once again, I realized how cunning Brice Wilson was. As long as he kept me in limbo and the crew guessing as to my ultimate disposition, I was really no threat to him.

"Captain, Mr. Sandborn is here." The watch officer reported my presence to Wilson.

"Thank you, Captain, for allowing me on the bridge to see landfall."

"Don't thank me, Mr. Sandborn. Thank Chief Steward Ariti. He pestered me no end to let you see this. My druthers would have been to leave you confined to quarters until a board could be convened. But Angie was persuasive if not a little ham handed. Sometimes you make a decision just to make the pestering go away."

"Well, in any regard, I am grateful, Captain. Thank you for whatever part you played in it. Where are we? What's our status?" I realized as those last words were coming out of my mouth that if Wilson wanted to, he could hear them as commands of a superior officer from a subordinate for a report. I had softened my voice and emphasized the question aspect of it all so I hoped he wouldn't. Fortunately he didn't.

"We're standing out about 1,500 kilometers in low planet orbit. In our current direction of travel and Debris' rotation, we should be able to see the entire planet in under 2 hours not that it will do us a heck of a lot of good visually. It is completely cloud enshrouded."

"Have you done an eco analysis? Are we going to be able to land and work?" Again, I was a little hesitant to push for information, but Wilson seemed content that I wasn't elbowing my way into his authority.

"We did that a day and a half ago as soon as we were close enough. It's a Class M[3], roughly the same size and mass as Earth. And I'm not sure how, but in spite of the fact this is a rogue planet with no star to radiate it, the temperatures are well within our ability to tolerate them. We may even be able to go out without a suit. Initial atmospheric gas composition tests show a little above 18% oxygen and the rest inert, benign elements, so on the surface it'll be like breathing on a mountain top, but doable."

"That's incredible! It can support life? And here I was worried about an ice world with methane storms and an unstable geology. This is the best possible news!" I was ecstatic at this. To find a rogue planet was one thing and next to impossible. To find a habitable rogue planet is beyond impossible. And to find it within a two-week sub-luminal

---

[3] Obviously Sandborn did not use this term, and I would be very disappointed if you failed to recognize my tongue in cheek homage to Star Trek. But the truth is, the usage holds. Sandborn described Debris to me and it fits with the canon of Star Trek's planetary classifications. Class M - habitable by humans.

flight radius is like winning the lottery 50 times in a row.

"I'm assuming you didn't say anything about electronic transmissions of any kind because you didn't pick up any."

"We didn't."

I stayed on the bridge for the two hour transit around the planet. Wilson was right. There was nothing to see visually, but our penetrating sensors were able to roughly map out surface features. We didn't need much. We were self sufficient for repairs. We just needed a large, flat area to land and work.

There was also the chance that we might pick up low level radio or other electronic wave transmissions that were too weak for our earlier probe. If we did it would be a sure sign of sapient life. But even at this short range our sensors confirmed: Debris was silent.

While I hadn't held out any hope for intelligent life, it was still disappointing that a planet with a habitable eco system like Debris didn't have any.

"Wait! Run the output of that last scan again...reference around record point 13.8." Wilson's voice was urgent. "Sandborn, take a look at this and tell me what you think."

I edged closer to the view screen. The output was digital not photographic so it required some interpretation. Clearly we were looking at a large, flat area...a plain the size of probably Connecticut or Massachusetts back home. But there was this one aberration, smack dab in the middle. It looked like a choppy area of small to medium size hills of impossible inclines.

"Mr. Wilson, I can't say for sure, but none of that fits the geology. That has to be something other than any geologic force I know."

"Like what, Deke?"

"I don't want to say, Brice. What I'm thinking it looks like is too fantastic to even consider. It has to be a natural formation. The alternative is just too far out to consider."

"Like man made?"

"Jesus, Brice. As weird as that would be, I can't deny that's an option."

"Yeah. That's what I thought, too. Too weird to be that. But I've got nothing else." Brice paused and I could see him biting the inside of his check. "Chief Miller, make for a landing point immediately outside that aberration. Put us down on the flattest surface in the area."

"Aye, Captain."

Turning to me, Wilson cast a wary eye. "Deke, I know what you're thinking, but our first and only priority is to repair the jump drives. We are a cargo ship, not a science vessel. We have neither the crew nor the equipment for race contact."

"Then why are you putting down there?"

"Because it's the most level area I've seen in the scans, and it appears to be grassy so we can see anything unusual coming at us for kilometers in any direction."

"And?"

"Deke, there is no 'and' here. Whatever that anomaly is, and it could be a castle from Earth for all I care, we've got no time or crew for exploration."

The subject was closed. Brice turned back to managing the landing process and I faded into the background behind the bustle of the unusual routine of landing a space craft on a planet with gravity and terrain rather than simply space docking. Without command or responsibility I was at best an unnecessary annoyance.

But I wasn't going anywhere until I could get a glimpse of whatever that aberration was. He may not have the time for exploration, but I sure did. In fact, I had that in abundance.

Suddenly the computer's soothing female voice rose above the activity: "Warning, hull temperatures exceeding 1,500 degrees Celsius. Hull failure likely. Hull failure likely."

CHAPTER 5 - **Into the Darkness**

"Chief! Switch to manual! Adjust entry angle down by degrees!" Wilson was genuinely alarmed.

"Aye, sir. Switching to manual. I have the yoke. Attack angle 40 degrees. Adjusting down by degrees…39 degrees… 38 degrees."

"Slower, Chief. Let's not skip out. We can always come around again if we do, but I'd rather stick this the first time." Wilson was right. The real danger was an attack angle too steep and we'd burn up from friction or be crushed from the drag.

"Aye, sir. Slowing adjustments."

I couldn't see the hull temperature gauge from where I was, but I knew every eye on the bridge that could focus on it was focused on it. The Rapacious was not intended for atmospheric entry and so did not have more than minimal heat shielding.

Wilson grabbed the intercom. "All hands, this is the Captain. Looks like we may have a bumpy ride to the surface. Stow loose objects and brace yourselves."

The atmosphere must be denser than we anticipated. We needed to make our angle of attack more shallow. But if the angle is too shallow, the ship will simply bounce off the atmosphere back into space. With this dense an atmosphere, the problem is not coming around again, but rather if there can be an entry at all. The denser the atmosphere the smaller the entry corridor, the space between burning up and bouncing off.

"Chief, on my mark, hold angle of attack." Wilson was "steering" by using the hull temperature gauge. It had stopped increasing and was holding steady. It needed to decrease. As soon as it got back below 1500 degrees, that would be just slightly less than the maximum attack angle the ship could stand. But would it be steep enough to allow us to continue down to the surface? And if we couldn't reach the surface, we were condemned.

"Mark!"

"Aye, sir. Holding entry at 37.25 degrees."

"Increase angle of attack to 37.35 degrees and hold it as steady as you can, Chief."

"Aye, Captain."

Now all eyes switched to the altimeter. If the angle of attack was enough, it should be moving downward. If it stayed the same, we'd essentially be in orbit, but unable to go any lower, barred from the surface. If it increased, we were bouncing off the atmosphere and back into space.

It took agonizing seconds, but the digital readout began to slowly tick downwards. We were going to be able to descend. You could feel a corporate sigh of relief from the bridge crew.

"Chief, mind the hull temperature. Adjust the attack angle to maintain just under 1500 degrees. We need to make sure we maximize the breaking effect of the atmospheric drag to slow us down to landing speed."

"Aye, sir."

Chief Miller was a savvy crew member...arrogant, but with the skills and knowledge to back up his arrogance. You may not like him, but you probably wanted him at the controls. The "dance" with the atmosphere was just beginning. There would be ongoing adjustments of the attack angle both up and down. But once our rate of descent was at "landing speed", our thrusters could take over and finish the decent.

For the first time since the alarm, we could actually afford to take our eyes off the controls and look out the bridge portals.

Slowly but inexorably the stone black sky began to lighten ever so slightly. Debris was covered with clouds and there was no external light source like our sun, but it was undeniable that the black was giving way to dark gray. The clouds we were descending through became more visible. At first it was just lighter flashes in the midst of the dark of space. But then those flashes became more steady and themselves were interrupted by still lighter flashes[4].

Within minutes we were below the cloud canopy and we caught our first glimpse of the terrain. There was a gasp from some of the bridge crew nearest the viewport. What revealed

---

[4] At no point in the descent did it ever become light. In fact on Debris, it never got much lighter than a pre-dawn on Earth. But as to that initial descent, Sandborn had some difficulty in describing this progression. As best I could understand it, it seemed to be like the change in light between the darkest hours of night and the time in the very, very early morning where all you can see are the silhouettes of objects, but not their textures or colors. It is still dark in those hours, but just not as dark. Bear in mind that this description of Debris' vista from clouds to ground is my own best reconstruction of what was difficult for Sandborn to describe in great detail.

itself to us was a vista which looked like seeing the lights of Earth at night from high Earth orbit, only we were much closer than that. But still the resemblance to an Earth at night was startling.

Networks of light sprang out from larger, more luminescent hubs. In some cases those hubs were connected by a single or double long "arm". In other cases, those hubs and spokes were isolated from others by wide patches of darkness. We were descending into a patchwork of luminescence.

The whole vista was lit by an eerie glow, originating from the ground but reflected faintly by the dense cloud canopy. We were entering a cloaked alien planet with its own captive light source. Instead of light streaming down from a sun, light glowed up from the ground…a dark, shadowless world that was itself a shadow.

Thus, by this first utterly fantastic view, Debris was indelibly etched into my mind. It was simultaneously both early dawn and late evening.

With some disappointment I realized that it was going to be impossible for anyone to see the aberration in the darkness.

We landed without further incident. It seemed almost anticlimactic given all that we had been through. Before anyone could exit the ship, a series of detailed tests needed to be conducted to determine the suitability of the environment for use. We had our longer range scans and probes, but there was no substitute for in situ readings. Over the centuries we had come 180 degrees away from our original fear of alien organisms and strange diseases, but there were still some good reasons for doing a battery of tests to screen out potential life threatening elements. Humans had proven to be largely resilient to unique, non-terrestrial organisms. Most of the tests had to do with chemicals rather than viruses or bacteria. Methane is a biggie. It is non-toxic to humans, but in sufficient quantities in otherwise breathable atmosphere it can crowd out oxygen in your lungs and you can literally suffocate.

Realistically it was going to take about 6 hours to do a thorough job. We could just put on environmental suits, but if we could do the work without them the time required would be cut by a third. Plus we could also use the time to renew the onboard oxygen exchangers, take care of certain waste issues, and figuratively open the windows and blow the stink out. Having breathable, temperate air available was a real boon.

Wilson detailed the watch officer and the two crew members on bridge watch to conduct the testing. He then made a ship wide announcement calling a halt to all non-essential work and ordering all hands not on watch or doing essential tasks to quarters. Once the environmental tests were done, he wanted as many of the crew as possible as rested as possible to take on the repair task.

As the extra crew filed off the bridge, I found myself next to Wilson.

"Aren't you a little more curious about that anomaly now that we're safe on the surface?"

"No, Sandborn. I'm not. And I'm not totally convinced we are safe on the surface. I didn't command the crew to quarters for a beauty sleep. This air may turn out to be perfectly safe to breathe, but that doesn't mean this place is perfectly safe to occupy."

"Aye, sir. What do you want me to do?"

"I want you to go to your rack and sleep if you can. Or don't sleep. I really don't care. I don't trust you, Deke, as far as I could throw you. I don't think you deliberately killed Ahriman, but I don't think you are entirely innocent either. So until I know where on that spectrum you really fall, I'm certainly not going to expose myself or the crew to you or you to them. The crew thinks confining you to quarters is probably overkill, so I'm not going to require that. But I am going to order you to stay the hell out of the way. I've got enough guys with enough skill to repair this thing. I don't need you, but I may. And if and when I do, I'll call you, but not before. So stay out of the way."

"Look, Brice, you and I both know that the real reason you don't want to use me has nothing to do with trust. You don't want to give me any pathway back to my position as First Mate because then I'll be captain and you won't. I get that. In fact, were I in your place, I'd probably do the exact same thing. But don't dress this up as being concerned for your safety or the crew's. This is strictly politics, plain and simple. I'll stay out of your way not because you're ordering me, but because, frankly, I think you're doing a pretty good job as captain. We're in a very difficult situation, might be unable to ever get home, and could die in any one of a hundred ways in space. But you got us to Debris safely, you've got a good sense of what the crew needs, and your approach to repairs (except for not using me) is sound. But understand this: the moment I think you're making bad decisions or putting my and the crew's lives in danger unnecessarily, you bet I'm going to step up and say something. And if that results in you losing your precious captain's position, so be it. I'm not going to die out here because of your ego, mismanagement, stupidity, or all three. So I'm staying out of the way for now because of my own decision, not your order. Are we clear, Brice?"

It was a risk confronting him like that. He could slap me back in my quarters with a lock on the door and a guard in the passageway. But my own political sense told me that Brice was getting just a tiny bit too cocksure of his position. I may be under confinement and relieved of duty, but shipboard life was still a competition, and based on the crew's response to my confinement, I still had political cards to play. He needed to know that and be taken down a notch or two.

He stopped and turned toward me, putting a finger solidly on my sternum. "Deke, you try anything like that and not only will I hold a board of inquiry, I'll make it a full fledged trial. And I'll be your judge, jury, and if necessary executioner. Now are we clear, Deke?"

I slowly pushed his finger off my chest while making unblinking eye contact with him. "Brice, that's a bluff and you know it. The crew won't stand for it. They might not like me, but they don't really like you any better. Besides, my knowledge of this ship and its systems is greater than yours. If we're in danger, we're going to need expertise. The crew would not let you execute one of the biggest human assets you've got."

I paused a moment and then continued in a more congenial tone. "So take what I'm giving you, Brice. I'm telling you that as long as you're doing the right things at the right time in the right way, I'll stay out of your way. If you can do that, we both get what we want. You get to keep your position and I get out of this alive."

I could see he got the point. His shoulders slumped almost imperceptibly and he looked away and down. "Just stay out of the way, Deke."

There was no need to answer. I just turned and worked my way back to my quarters.

Angie was waiting for me. "Would you like something to eat, Mr. Sandborn?"

"No thanks, Angie. I think I'm going to hit the rack. Thank you for getting me that pass to the bridge. It accomplished way more than you thought."

"Is that a good thing, Mr. Sandborn?"

"Yes, I think so. The captain and I had a talk and I think we came to an understanding. I don't think much is going to change for me for the rest of this trip, assuming the repairs work out alright. But things should be a lot less tense. I suppose that was your real goal all along?"

"Mr. Sandborn, I'm just a mess rat. Such things are above my pay grade. Shall I wake you when the captain gives the all clear for external activities?"

"If I'm not already up, yes. And, Angie...mess rat or not, thank you for interceding on my behalf."

"You're welcome, Mr. Sandborn. Good night."

Six hours later Angie was knocking at my quarters with a steaming cup of joe. I had slept well, but awoke with a sense of anticipation. For what, I had no idea. I thought back to the academy and our junior year training cruise to the moon. It was the first time I had ever set foot off Earth and like any 20 year old, I was pumped. When we arrived at the academy base, I could not wait to set foot on alien soil. I remember how disappointed I was. It was barren, boring, and lifeless. I don't know what I expected, but whatever it was, it wasn't there.

Debris was definitely not the moon. I'd seen that it had extensive light sources, and that could account for my anticipation. However, all my years of space travel had convinced me that reality rarely matched expectation and never matched imagination.

Then there was the anomaly. Well, I groused, there was also a man in the moon, but that disappeared the closer you got. This would, too. It would be a geologic formation of unexpected, maybe even unexplained causes, but it would be utterly natural...and boring.

"Angie, have you heard the results of the enviro-analysis?"

"Yes sir. Earth normal with a couple of variances. The captain has approved suitless egress. The air density is a bit higher, oxygen percentage a bit lower, temps are roughly the equivalent of a brisk fall morning in the mountains, humidity neither moist nor dry. All in all, it is going to feel pretty comfortable if you're dressed right. And gravity is about 90% of Earth."

"Are the hatches open yet?"

"Yes sir. They opened about 30 minutes ago."

"OK. Thanks Angie. I think I'm going to go out, stretch my legs, and check out the neighborhood."

It took me a few minutes to collect a com-link, a coat, work gloves, and a heavy wrench. We are a cargo ship after all, and have no weapons to speak of…so a heavy wrench would have to suffice if I met any hostile…I don't know what… hostile anythings!

Feeling at least marginally equipped, I made my way to the bottom most hatch. My first glimpse of the planet was looking down through the opening. I could see the ground immediately below and it was charred and barren from our landing rockets.

Setting foot on the ladder I descended. When I reached the bottom rung, stepped off and turned around, I was not prepared for what I saw.

CHAPTER 6 - **Darkness**

A black and gray world. A world devoid of color. A world of shapes without definition. A world with the energy of day, but at night. Utterly fantastical yet strikingly real.

It was all these things all at the same time. It struck me as though some grand designer had taken everything you didn't know you assumed about Earth and turned them upside down and inside out. As strange as it sounds, it felt like it does when you meet a childhood friend decades later and find they are both changed and the same. It was like meeting Earth in another, older form.

Let me start again. I turned around to see a nighttime scene of a field of waist high grass extending into the distance in every direction. The field was alive from the motion of the breeze upon the grass, causing it to bend and bow, turn and curl…in waves starting where I was standing and marching into the distance of my vision. It was mesmerizing.

It reminded me of modern dancers on Earth, bending and swaying with the music, only this was millions of tiny dancers moving in perfectly unfolding synchrony. And as they turned and twined in waves, every shade of gray and black imaginable could be seen in them.

You never think of gray and black being colors in themselves. They are the absence of color, the stage just before color appears and right after color disappears. But this…. This was a world in which the whole spectrum of colors were expressed in the darkest of grays and blacks.

Had someone told me about it, I would have thought it to be dull. This was anything but. It was as though I had never seen color before.

I could not see far in the darkness before the grays and blacks melded into sameness. My mind kept telling me it was soon to be light…or dark. On Earth, the light is always moving from dark and then back to the dark again, and with it colors from blacks to grays to colors back to grays and blacks. We humans have been conditioned to expect the change, to anticipate the waxing and waning of light and color. More importantly, we have been conditioned to not expect light and color to remain the same from hour to hour. The only real trust we have of light and color is that it is always changing.

Here was Debris, a world that was forever in pre-dawn, never to see dawning of light; or in a trick of perspective, it was forever in gathering darkness never to see the full dark of night. Such light and color I was seeing had been that way for millennia and would be that way for millennia to come.

I realized this awareness of the sameness of the light and shadows almost immediately. It did not take long to sink in. On Earth we would sit and watch the dusk gather, and you could actually trace the growth of darkness. It did not happen in hours, but seemingly in minutes. The change was observable and notable. It could be watched if one was just patient enough.

Here, it was the lack of change that was so discernible. As

the minutes went by, the lack of change in the quantity and quality of the light became cumulatively noticeable. The truth dawned that this was day, night, and everything in-between on Debris. And I realized it was not disappointing or depressing. To the contrary, it was exhilarating. Here was a place that was not limited by either light or dark. There was no sense that if you started something you would only have a certain amount of time before you had to quit. The sense of consistency awoke a strange perspective that truly anything was possible here. Because it was not wholly either, strangely it was both. Had it been only day, one would have felt stuck in the fullness of day...the same for the dead of night. But here in the in-between, the potential of both day and night existed simultaneously, in harmony, without seam.

On Debris, it almost seemed like time itself had been eternally paused, as if in the distant past, on one particular day, a day like any other, as the world was getting darker and heading into night; some great and divine hand had just pushed the pause button.

All of this hit me in a rush. It wasn't an unfolding understanding. It was a sudden realization. I knew it all at once, like when you come to know something in a moment, you feel you should have known (and probably did) all along. Meaning springs full-blown into your mind.

I walked out into the field of waving grass feeling an actual breeze on my flesh. After the recycled air on the Rapacious, it was an almost sensual feeling. It was chilly and had I not put on a coat, I would have been cold. I could feel the beginning of goosebumps on my forearms. The air had a faint smell to it, slightly spicy, almost sour, but in a pleasant way. It reminded me of something I had either smelled or tasted before, but I could not put my finger on it.

I broke off a blade of grass and rubbed it between my fingers and instantly the smell intensified. It was like the smell of fresh bread, fresh rye bread. It smelled of caraway.

Looking up I peered into the distance. In the darkness I could see maybe a kilometer, but so much of night vision depends on there being a light source where you are looking. Sure, in a night sky you can see a galaxy that's 2.5 million light-years away. But in the dark, with no major light source, we often infer the reality of the dark things we dimly see at night from what we know from seeing during the day. Sure we may see things up close, but from a distance we infer what things are rather than seeing them.

Here on Debris, an utterly alien world, there was no point of reference to infer from except for what I brought with me from Earth. I could see the waving grass clearly for almost a kilometer because it is familiar and Earth-like. But there were other shadows out there that I could see for which I had no frame of reference to know what they were.

I knew I had 5 or 6 hours before I needed to check back to the ship...not that they would miss me. Quite the contrary. Except for Angie, no one knew or cared where I was. No, I needed to check back because it was likely if the repairs went quicker than expected, I would be inadvertently stranded on Debris. That would not do.

Walking toward the distant shadowy shapes, I picked up my pace. Perhaps I was wary of taking too much time away from the ship. But really I was just plain excited. Those shapes were undoubtedly the anomaly Wilson and I had seen on the scanning orbit. We were supposed to land near them, only Chief Miller was given some discretion as the pilot. Had I been Miller, I'd have landed in the safest spot, which would have been away from unknowns, three or four kilometers at least. It appeared that was exactly what he'd done.

It's difficult to judge distances on an alien world because you just don't have anything familiar to judge by. So, there only being one way to find out, I made a bee line for them. If

I didn't reach them in 2 hours, I'd turn around and retrace my steps. If it took longer than 2 hours to get there, it was pointless as I would have no time to explore.

Had I been in a milder climate I would have been sweating my pace was such, but not here. In about 30 minutes I was able to see the shapes with some level of discrimination. I could see they were many individual things in various shapes and sizes instead of just one or a few large and oddly shaped things. They were definitely constructed and not natural formations. It was too soon to say they were buildings, but I couldn't think what else they might be.

In 45 minutes I could begin to discriminate the separation between those in the foreground and those behind. Also, details began to emerge...what I took to be roofs, windows, and doors. Clearly these were constructed structures of some kind. I could see no movement, no artificial light of any kind: there were no noises of any kind other than the wind and grass.

By the time I reached the outlying structures, it was clear whatever this was had been abandoned. For how long I had no clue at this point. It could have been as recent as our landing. The light of our landing rockets and the resultant fire they caused in the caraway grass would have lit the place up. It could have scared the inhabitants into hiding.

Or it could have happened eons ago.

The structures were, for the most part, single story. There were some I could see that might have been multi-stories, but not more than two; at the most three. They were sophisticated in construction, not like mud or grass huts or other primitive buildings. There were some that appeared to be wood, others metal, still others an opaque glass like substance. Judging by the doorway size and window placements, I surmised the inhabitants were roughly humanoid is size and shape. Well, the humanoid part was a guess, but it was clear that whatever they were, they were roughly the same height and girth as a humanoid. The handle placement suggested grasping appendages, and the thresholds a standard stride.

To this point I had seen no sign of animal life anywhere. The structures were all dark and appeared empty. The first few structures I encountered I stopped, listened outside, and then went up to the windows to see if I could see anything.

This sounds casual and all, like I just walked up, knocked on the door, and asked, "Anybody home?" To the contrary, I practiced some old hunting skills and quickly went down wind and moved furtively and carefully from cover to cover to get close enough to listen for signs of life. I had no idea if there were "people" there or not, or if there were, if they were rational and peaceful beings.

The outlying structures appeared to be dwellings. Outside, if there had been any landscaping or personalization, it was all gone. The grass had grown up to and around the houses. Inside there were what appeared to be various types and sizes of chairs, tables, and other furniture, all that would accommodate humanoid beings. I sat in one or two of the chairs and they weren't uncomfortable. If they were humanoid, they may have been about my height, but their legs would have been longer and their torsos shorter.

There was undisturbed dust everywhere. That answered one question: at least the outlying dwellings were not recently occupied. I started moving towards what I perceived as the center of "town". I guess it was a town.

As I moved inward, I was less and less cautious as edifice after edifice proved to be long vacant. The center was a large square, maybe about an acre in size of what appeared to be paving stones and dotted with benches and statuary.

It was my first look at what the inhabitants of this world were like. Indeed they were long legged and short bodied.

Their arms were also disproportionately long, reaching to what I assumed were their knees.

The face was striking. Almost owl-like with large, open eyes, a sharp nose and a small mouth. I supposed the eyes were an evolutionary adaptation to the low light levels. There were no ears that I could see, and no hair on the head. They appeared almost bald.

The statues were uniformly clothed in loose fitting tunics that covered their torsos. And while a sleeveless tunic made little sense in a world that was perennially chilly, where "skin" was visible there appeared to be a covering of feathers. They were not large feathers, like one might expect for flight. They were not "plumage" as one might expect if the purpose was to discriminate one being from another. They were small, closely "knit", layered, and provided a substantial covering. The effect was more like fur than feathers, but they were definitely feathers.[5]

I could not judge size by the statues because they were of all different sizes themselves, so the scale was impossible to know.

It was clear they were humanoid, intelligent, and even artistic. The inscriptions on the statues were indecipherable to me, but it was clear they were conveying information about the individual. Where on Earth, at least some of the statues would have had martial overtones, none of these did. With few exceptions, the likeness was engaged in some type of activity with what appeared to be writing implements or

---

[5] Certain readers may note, as did I, a striking similarity with "Sorns", one of the three races of humanoids from Mars, in C.S. Lewis' book, <u>Out of the Silent Planet</u>. I certainly was taken aback by it and questioned Sandborn about it. He had heard of Lewis but had not read any of his works. I had supposed Lewis' work to be entirely his own fiction, but this brings that assumption into question.

tools I took to represent various occupations. There were no statues that I could discern that had any reference to military matters…certainly none were astride a horse, even assuming this race had something like horses.

I turned from the park to survey the surrounding buildings. Mostly they were of stone construction, two stories mostly. They appeared to be public buildings with wider doors and windows. One building caught my eye in particular. It was made of that opaque glass and was essentially windowless. I assumed it was a bank or other type of institution that would have required some security. I decided to check it out because it was so different from the other buildings.

Entering the building, I found a single chair set in the middle of the spacious and open first floor. It was curious. It was the first thing I had seen in all this clearly meant for comfort. It was also set securely into the floor. On Earth I would have said it was a 20th century barber's chair. But, clearly, for a people covered with feathers, it could not be that. Attached to nothing but the floor, it had no wires or other electrical connections, and was without art or filigree. I decided it was safe to try out and stepped up on the footrest and swung my body into the seat, leaning back with my head square in the headrest.

It was very comfortable and seemed to accommodate itself to my body. I relaxed, let out the breath that I realized I'd been holding, and looked up. The ceiling was plain with just a simple geometric pattern which I realized was inexplicably receding from me and getting more and more out of focus. Strange. I had no sense of movement.

Then two things happened almost simultaneously. First, every warning bell in my head went off telling me I was in danger. Second, I lost consciousness.

Chapter 7 - **Out of Darkness**

Dear Reader,

Sandborn's time in the chair was impossible for him to relate to me in practical terms. I pressed him for details, but he couldn't give me any. Detail escaped him. The work of the chair was internal, not external. He felt more than he saw. He experienced emotional content rather than physical. It was as though the chair bypassed his body and mind and worked solely through his heart. Not the blood pump, mind you, but the heart in the way one speaks of the heart of a matter or a man; the core, the essential center or spirit of the thing. To him it was the most profound experience imaginable. In fact, it was almost indescribable except in the most elusive terms.

The best he could do was to talk about what it was like, not what it was. We quickly realized how impossible it would be to reduce the experience to words, so we decided not even to try. Instead, we experimented with various scenarios that might be evocative enough to give you an inkling of what happened to him.

What follows does not hold a candle to what he experienced, but it is the best we could do.

# # #

I slowly recovered and found myself no longer in the chair. Somehow, I had been transported to the engineer's compartment of a bullet train. I was alone in the cabin, a hand on a throttle, my foot on a dead man's brake. The train speedometer showed the train traveling at over 300 kmh. I've never driven a train before, certainly not a terrestrial bullet train. At first it was exhilarating, traveling at such speed at the controls of such a machine, the engine throbbing behind me, the track racing beneath me.

As the wonder subsided and my immediate surroundings became more familiar, I realized I had no idea how to regulate the speed or apply the brakes of this behemoth. The controls were incomprehensible to me. No matter what switch I flipped or lever I threw, it had no effect whatsoever on direction or speed. I even took my foot off the dead man's brake, but it made no difference. Either the train was out of control or I was totally ignorant of any of the ways to regulate it. This was not going to end well.

The terror started as a stone in the pit of my stomach. At first, it was a feeling of anger at my inability to find the right lever, but it soon began to morph into a powerlessness that nothing I seemed to do had any effect, then to anxiety as I realized the likely outcome, and finally to outright fear as I became convinced of that outcome. I was alone. There was no solution.

And then I saw it. Like a mirror image, a train, a bullet train, moving at an equal speed, in the distance but coming in the opposite direction. I was not following it. It was coming towards me. With my eyes I traced the track I was on toward the horizon only to see it was the same track the mirror image was on.

I frantically redoubled my efforts to stop my train. I was going entirely too fast to jump without killing myself, but if I couldn't avoid the oncoming train I was going to die either way. At a closing speed of 600 kph, the distance between us was shrinking at almost 170 meters a second. I literally was doing the math in my head, and I had seconds to live.

Suddenly time slowed way down. My movements seemed languid. I had all the time in the world to try anything and everything. Still nothing made any difference. But in slow motion I had a seemingly infinite amount of time to consider my fate. My helplessness became an unendurable weight.

As the moments passed, I began to see details in almost everything. I could see the dirt on the glass face of the dials. I could pick out the rough edges of the control panel. I could even begin to see the paint pattern on the approaching train. Seeing with that level of clarity did nothing to ameliorate the terror. In fact, it multiplied it. I don't know what the level above terror is, but I experienced it.

I was going to die.

The collision was in slow motion, too. I saw the seconds before impact as minutes. I saw the hood begin to crumple and fold up, coming towards me. I could hear the scream of metal and plastic as it was literally torn into shreds by the impact. I felt myself beginning to lurch forward as the impact stopped the train's forward motion, but not mine. The bones in my cheek began to disintegrate as my head hit against the instrument panel. My chest bones snapped, and I could feel the shards puncturing my lungs. My legs dislocated as my upper body hit the panel flush, but there was nothing to stop my legs.

I felt consciousness slipping away from me, but not like passing out or falling asleep. My consciousness was being eaten by a cold blackness, a nothingness that literally consumed my mind and sense of who I was piece by piece. I was no longer Deke Sandborn, executive officer, maritime graduate; I was just a man. Then I was no longer a man. I was merely a person. Then I was merely a thought. Then I was merely no more.

My last memory was that I had no more memories. I was that cold blackness. There was nothing… and it lasted for an eternity. I cannot explain how you can experience nothing for an eternity, but I did. I was eternally soulless, numb, discorporate, and empty; devoid of any sense of who I was. I was nothing…an endless nothing.

# # #

Eventually eternity passed. As nothing gave way to something, as dark gave way to light, as cold gave way to warmth, I slowly awoke as from a long, dreamless night. I was still me. I had not died. I was not mangled. I was not in the darkness or the train. Eons ago, it seemed I had been in a chair on a strange, dark planet, but I was not there either.

Awareness crept into my consciousness. I had the sensation of wind blowing from my back. I was standing on a railing on a bridge in the sunlight. It was warm, like the first warm day of spring, and it felt so good after an eternity of dark, cold nothingness. I could see a wide gorge beneath me and a horizon a million miles away, or so it seemed. It was so good to be alive.

I tried to move back from the railing, to step down and away, but my feet would not move. When I looked down, I saw that my ankles and feet were bound and a strap of some kind attached. I recognized it: a bungee strap. I turned to see and get help, but at that moment a gust of wind, something, or someone tipped me towards the abyss. I could feel myself losing my balance and falling forward.

Questions of how I got there, what was going on, or anything else that had been in my head vanished in the face of the feeling of falling. I had heard of bungee jumping, but had never done it. It seemed like a foolhardy thing to do for a rush. But here I was, tipping past the point of regaining my balance, about to do my first bungee jump ever.

I tried to turn back and grab the railing, but I had fallen too far. I rotated back to face what was rushing up to meet me. There was no safety net, no river, no bay, only rocky escarpment.

For the second time, my senses downshifted and moments became minutes. I looked up and saw the cord drawing taut. I looked down and did some mental calculations. I would be fine. There was a margin of safety apparently built in. The free fall I was in would end. I would stop by slowing degrees as the cord stretched to its limits and then rise as the elastic contracted. I would be fine.

I felt the cord grow taut and stretch. I felt my speed decrease, but not as much as I would have liked. I heard the "crack" as the cord snapped in two just above my ankles. I felt my speed accelerate impossibly fast.

A stray thought suddenly elbowed its way into my mind: "The terminal velocity of a human body dropped from height on Earth is 200 kph." It infuriated me that of all things, my mind could be nonchalant in the midst of this.

Time stayed dilated. I could see the ground coming up towards me, and the outcome was unavoidable. Again the fear and powerlessness flooded my consciousness. This time there was an added agony, that of futility. In the train at least I had switches, levers, and pedals to operate. They turned out to be useless, but at least I had the illusion of potential control. Here there was literally nothing I could do. All my intelligence, strength, learning; anything I had valued in my life as a competitive advantage was of no value. I did not differ from a stone. A living, feeling, self-aware stone, but a stone nonetheless.

There is some reflex that takes over at such times, regardless of how pointless it may be. I tucked my chin to my chest and rolled my shoulders. I flipped in slow motion on to my back. Better to hit back to, I reasoned, only to realize there was no reason to it. Back to, face to…what did it possibly matter? Was I afraid to face the inevitable? Was it better to let it take me by surprise? There was no lessening of terror either way.

After all, there was no question I was going to die. It was the terror I was trying to escape. There is that part of every human being that never gives up trying to control some aspect of our situation. Even faced with death, we tempt ourselves with the illusion that we are going to face death stoically; that we are going to die, but we are going to have a death on our terms. Inevitably, there comes that moment, as where I was now, when we realize the futility of thinking we are somehow powerful enough to wrestle anything from death.

It was my spine that hit the rocks first. I had the sensation of pain over my entire body simultaneously. I felt my spine unroll and my hips hit the rocks, and the shiver of bone on rock went simultaneously to my feet and my head.

Breath was forced from my lungs as my body flattened. My arms and legs which had been extended upward, were the next to hit. All four simultaneously broke and hyper-extended, tearing vessels, cartilage, and nerves, adding to the already unbearable pain.

Then my head hit, and the sound was just what they said in the movies: it sounded like a melon hitting the pavement. It was a sickening thud. I heard it. Things moved that slowly.

My sight was lost, replaced by a pulsing red flash.

The pain had reached a crescendo. I cried out in a rage against the agony. But at that moment, I was utterly undone, for no sound came out. I was without breath. I could not even rage.

The blackness began once more. I found myself stripped again of my identity, then my understanding, and at last my awareness.   The cold dark I was infinitely familiar with swallowed me.   No...it digested me into pieces, and then those pieces into parts, and then those parts into nothing.

Unbodied and un-souled, I slipped into a second eternity of nothing.

# # #

How many eternities can a man survive? I know now, an infinite amount. He can survive them, but he cannot survive unchanged.

Each death was followed by an eternity of darkness. Each eternity of darkness was followed by another life. In each life I was powerless to avoid the inevitable death.   In each resurrection I found new life, but no way of escape. Each life was a real as real can be, or so it felt.   Each death was as profound as I had imagined death could be.   Each eternity was a true eternity, although I do not know how that could be.

When at last it was over, I found myself still seated in the chair looking at the geometric design on the ceiling above me. I had not moved, neither in location nor in position. It was as if I awoke from a nap.   But instead of being refreshed, the weight of an infinite number of eternities was on me. In the core of my being, I knew I had actually experienced every bit of everything that had happened. Everything was as real in the chair as everything that is real outside the chair.

I could no more call what I went through "a dream" then a soldier could call seeing his buddy shot "a dream". In his situation, the impact of the reality feels to be more than he can possibly bear, so he pushes it away by making it "dreamlike" in his mind. We do this because it enables us to distance ourselves from the weight of death. But for me, this was the opposite. Obviously, it had to be "a dream" because no significant time had passed, but my mind demanded I consider it real...as real as anything else in my life. I had no choice. It was real.

By degrees I returned to this timeline. My mind was flying trying to make sense of everything that had happened. I was still drifting back from an eternity of eternities to the present.

By degrees I began to see certain undeniable elements emerge. Death was inevitable. My ability to control that was non-existent. Nothing carried over from life into death.

By degrees, I began to put some pieces together. If life is futile, what is the point? If any life is merely a momentary pop-up of substance that is suddenly here and then gone in an eternity of nothingness, what value is it? If my life is that pop up, then what is the point of me?

By degrees a certain light began to dawn in my mind. In every life I was alone; I was totally dependent on myself. It was the way I lived my life. It was the way everyone lived their lives. In fact, it was so ingrained in my being that I would have never even noticed that was a consistency in every life I lived in the chair. I would never have noticed it except that I wondered if I had been with someone, would it have mattered? Would it have made a difference? Would they have helped me stay alive? And my instant mental retort was, "No. Why would they?"

"No. Why would they?" The thought echoed in my head. "Why would they?" "Why would they?" "Why would they?" And with every echo the answer came back. "They wouldn't". "They wouldn't." "They wouldn't."

By degrees the question in my head morphed from "Why would they?" to "Why wouldn't they?"

I had never faced that question before. I had no ready answer other than the childish, "They just wouldn't." "They just wouldn't." "They just wouldn't."

I had no patience with that part of myself. There is always an answer. I straightened myself mentally and insisted, "But WHY?" With that, the answer revealed itself with instant crystal clarity. "Because, in the same place, I wouldn't."

It was simultaneously clear and damning, the truth and a curse. The scales of justice in my own mind had weighed me and found me wanting. They would not have helped me because I would not have helped them.

The reality of that answer was a hot iron searing my soul. I temporized. "It would not have mattered. We both would have still died. There was no escape. It would have made no difference."

My rationalization was a last-ditch effort to protect myself from the full realization of the futility of my life. I knew it was a lie. I knew it was a lie the moment I said it. It would have mattered. It would have made a difference. We may not have changed the outcome, but we would not have died alone. We would have challenged death together, and in that moment, we would have beaten that cold dark nothingness with something. The eternity would have been a degree or two warmer for the shared kindnesses of looking toward a solution for all rather than one.

If at death we are empty, the eternity that follows is empty. But if at death we are filled with a life of caring and kindness, the eternity that follows is anything but empty. Things did carry over from life to death.

Tears rolled down my cheeks. I was undone. I was alone. And somehow I would change that.

CHAPTER 8 - **Into the Light**

"Mr. Sandborn, are you alright?"

It was the 15th time Angie had asked me that. Or maybe it was the 50th. I don't know. It was three days since I walked back to the ship from the chair, and I had not left my quarters since returning.

"Angie, I'm fine," I lied.

"No, Mr. Sandborn, you're not fine. You've not moved from your quarters in three days. You've never done that apart from being too sick to get out of your bunk in all the time I've known you. What's wrong?"

"Nothing, Angie. Nothing is wrong."

I knew I was going to have to talk about this. I had been going over my experience again and again the last three days, and while I knew what I wanted, I had no clue how to make it happen. I'd always figured out these things before. I'm a smart guy. I'd figure it out, eventually. I just needed to think more or harder or something.

Then it hit me. I was going about this all wrong. My "take away" from the chair was that I had lived my life by myself, for myself, and that was futile. It was a dead end road that spilled out into dark nothingness. I had understood the futility could only be changed by caring and kindness toward others. More specifically, working together to solve a life-threatening problem.

I didn't like that outcome. In fact, I hated it, especially when it first occurred to me coming out of the chair. But after an eternity of eternities generated by the alternative, I was ready to accept it as the truth.

Here I was trying to solve this by looking into myself for the answers, the meaning. What if this is my "chair moment" right now? What if this is the chair testing me to see if I've really learned something from the whole experience? I may not actually be sitting in the chair, but I had to ask myself what made this moment any different from any moment I had spent in the chair? I'm alive, but I am on the way to death as certain as any of those moments in the chair. Was I going to try to figure this out on my own? Or was I actually going to learn how to make room for others?

I had vowed to change because I had been changed. It is laughable how fast that vow had just disappeared on the walk back to the ship. Thinking I was changed was apparently good enough for me. Sure.

So I gritted my teeth and started again.

"Wait a minute, Angie. I'm sorry. You're right. Something is wrong and I'm not fine. I didn't want to talk about it until I figured it out, but I'm realizing that there are some things I cannot figure out by myself. And this is one…a big one."

Angie looked surprised and then slowly he smiled. He actually smiled. I'd never seen that before. He was always so self-contained. "I beg your pardon, Mr. Sandborn. I thought you just apologized for something. I'm sure I misunderstood." Sarcasm, that was new, too.

Then it was my turn to smile. "Angie, you've been a

consistent and excellent steward. You've served captains and first mates for years, but you've never ever showed the slightest bit of loyalty to any of them. You served them, but when they were replaced or moved on, you just transferred your services to the next person who filled the empty slot. In all those years was there never any person, even just one, for whom you felt the slightest sense of loyalty? Has there been anyone that you've felt like you might have followed had they been willing to have you?"

"No, sir."

"Not even one?"

"No, sir. Not even one. Mr. Sandborn, you know that's not how things work. In this life if you become beholden to one man, you set yourself up to be used for his benefit and then turned out when it's no longer to his advantage to have you around. No, that's a sucker's life.

"Mr. Sandborn, I told you sometime ago that you are a fair man and I wasn't lying. You are as arrogant and selfish as the next man, and you'll do what you need to do to get ahead. Some men will set someone up to fail and then take advantage of it, like Captain Ahriman did to just about everybody. Other men will take advantage of another man's one time error, like Captain Wilson did to you. But I've never seen you do either one. Do you know how many men are like that? None, sir. At least none that I've ever seen.

"That makes you a fair man in my book, and a unique one in my experience. Maybe you might think that qualifies you for some sort of special relationship with me or the crew. Well, Mr. Sandborn, you may be fair, but you're still in it for yourself just like everyone else. And when it suits you, you'll move on with only a care for what's best for you. That qualifies you for nothing, sir. The only loyalty any smart man has is to himself."

Angie took a breath and waited for a response as I

struggled to find the right words. I had never done what I was about to do, and I had no idea what the outcome would be.

"Angie, I know that's the way things are. I'm just starting to wonder if that's the way things should be."

"That's crazy talk, Mr. Sandborn. No one talks about what should or shouldn't be. This is a starship, and the only talk that matters is what is and isn't. Space makes us all face facts. Out here, a man doesn't live or die by what ought to be. He lives or dies by what is and what isn't."

"Yes, Angie, I get that. But what if there was another way to work together? What if there was a way for a ship and its crew to get the job done better, quicker, safer, and…well…" I just trailed off, failing to find adequate words.

"Are you saying that what's wrong with you is that you have gone pie-eyed about some theoretical concept of 'how things ought to be'? C'mon, Mr. Sandborn."

"Angie, how long was I gone the other day when I left the ship?"

"A couple of hours at most. Why?"

"What if I told you I was gone for longer than that? Way longer than that? Like a lifetime? Like multiple lifetimes?"

"I'd say you were lying or crazy, sir."

"I'm neither, Angie. To you, I was gone a couple of hours. But something happened to me while I was gone that I can't begin to understand or explain, I lived multiple lifetimes in the blink of an eye. I'm not asking you to believe it. I'm just asking you to hear me out."

"Why?"

"Because I think I'm never going to understand this without telling someone else about it. I think it is something I'm not supposed to understand on my own. Angie, as strange as this sounds, I think I need you to help me understand all this."

"You need me? Mr. Sandborn, now I know this is all crazy talk. You've never needed anyone. Look, in some ways you're different, I'll admit; but in this way you are exactly like any officer I've ever worked for: you don't need anyone. What's your angle, sir? I feel like I'm being asked to believe something that is just going to suck me in and set me up."

"I know, Angie. That's exactly what it sounds like. And I know exactly how you feel. It's how I'd feel were I in your place. But it has taken me three days to figure out that I can't figure it out. That ought to give you a clue. If I were simply trying to use you for some advantage, why would I have waited three days? And what possible advantage could I gain? I'm under house arrest, accused of murder, and I can't see any way I can benefit from sucking you in to some plan.

"I give you my word that I will not ask you to do anything, give anything, promise anything. All I'm asking is for you to hear me out and then give me your opinion of what I'm saying. After that, you can call me crazy or stupid or whatever and walk away."

"I'll tell you what, Mr. Sandborn. You seem sincere and reasonably sane. Up to now you've never asked me for anything outside my normal duties. So you start telling me your tale and I'll listen. But the moment I think you're pulling a fast one, I'm out. I mean literally out. I'm walking out and the conversation is over, never to be picked up again. Agreed?"

"Agreed. Thank you, Angie."

So began what I ever after called "The Talk." I told him about the houses and the village and the statues. I told him about the building and the chair. Then I told him about everything: the train, the bungee, and every other life and death, the cold darkness, the agony, the loneliness, the helplessness, and finally the terror.

I unburdened my heart and my mind to him. In the

telling, it was like removing weight after weight off my soul…weights that I didn't even realize were there until they were gone. As I talked, I sensed a growing relief, a type of freedom.

Finally, I told him about waking from the chair and the terrible thoughts and memories of the aloneness. I told him what I realized about how none of those deaths would have been any different if I hadn't been alone, because even if there'd been another with me, neither of us would have helped the other.

I told him of my vow to change.

I talked for maybe three hours. Angie interrupted only occasionally to clarify a point or ask for an explanation of some remark. When I stopped, my quarters slowly filled with silence. Neither Angie nor I moved for minutes; me for just the feeling of relief, him I presume for the volume of what I told him. Then Angie took a deep breath.

"Mr. Sandborn, I don't know what to make of all this. I understand the words you spoke, and I get the pictures of the realities you experienced. But the whole point of it escapes me. I'm willing to assume everything you just told me is the truth and really happened to you. You have no proof, mind you. I only have your word that it happened. Still, why would you make up such a tale? So I have to assume you at least think you're telling the truth.

"I keep thinking of those statues of the creatures that presumably lived here and are no more. From how you described them, they seemed like reasonably intelligent beings with a head for learning and inventing and the like. Why would they make such a thing as this chair? What would be the purpose of having an invention that tricks you into thinking you're dead or dying over and over again? What would be the value of having a person endure an endless number of eternities? And may I add that the whole idea of an endless number of eternities makes my head hurt.

"I could see a chair that was like a library. I could see a chair that made you think you were on a distant planet living a whole lifetime among alien people when it was really only a minute. What an opportunity to learn about that in such detail.

"I could see a chair that taught you a lifetime of musical instrument lessons in, what did you call it, the blink of an eye? Think of it! You could sit down a complete novice one minute, and the next, wake up a virtuoso in any instrument you chose.

"There are so many possibilities for educating and training a person it boggles my mind. But to make the chair an engine of death and eternal darkness seems a terrible waste to me."

He was right, of course. Had humans made the chair it would have been an organ of intelligence and learning. But for how long? Would the human desire to be entertained and diverted, some entrepreneur would have converted the chair to an organ of sensation and satisfaction. I expressed this to Angie.

Then another thought occurred to me. "Angie, what if the chair isn't responsible for what happens? What if the chair simply responds to what we bring to it? What if the chair somehow knew that my greatest need was to overcome the inherent self centeredness of my life. I mean, it definitely has the ability to manipulate virtually every element in my body and mind, making a virtual reality be identical in every way except time to actual reality. Is it possible that such technology also has the ability to read us first, determine what is missing and then construct a reality around that?"

"I suppose so, Mr. Sandborn, but it doesn't really fit. Of all the lives you lived as you described them to me, there were only two things every one had in common: death and a cold, dark eternity. Now at the end you realized that if there had been another person with you and you had worked to save them rather than yourself, it would have carried over something into that cold, dark eternity. So that tells me that the only real constant in all your lives was death.

"No, Mr. Sandborn. I suspect the chair brings death, and a death that leads to eternity at that. I don't know if you have any religion. I don't. But even I know that death either leads to eternity or nothing…and nothing is just a different form of eternity. So this chair of yours is bringing real death. At least it seems to me, that's the point: to experience real death."

Suddenly the pieces began to assemble themselves in my mind. I went through countless different ways to die to come to the exact same place every time: death. I experienced countless eternities and all were the same: cold, dark nothingness. The eternities made the deaths real to me. Had there not been the empty eternity after each one, I would have just thought I was passing out and coming to, or sleeping and waking from so many dreams. But the eternities…they only follow real death. Angie was absolutely right. The chair brought real death, but with it the chance to get up and walk away from it.

A second chance! That's it!

"Angie, you're incredible. The chair was showing me the ultimate end of my life. It was showing me the sum total of what my life was worth…an empty eternity of nothing. And then the chair was giving me a second chance.

"It all fits. Death is the final arbiter of all things. Death shows us whether our lives are lived in value or not. But with actual death, by the time we realize it, it is too late to do anything about it.

"The point of the chair is just what you said, to bring death, because only in death can we truly see the real value or futility of life. The brilliance of the chair is that you experience death, and eternal death at that, without actually dying. You get to see what you did wrong and you get a second chance to do it right."

CHAPTER 9 - **Starting Over**

"LOOK OUT!"

I was screaming and running toward a group of three men standing outside, next to the jump drive ejection port. One of the men was Brice Wilson. In the night breeze and the rustle of the grass, they could not hear me.

"MOVE!!! MOVE!!!"

I dove headlong, full speed into the group with my arms spread wide. My momentum carried them several yards from where they were standing and knocked them to the ground in a heap. Captain Wilson was the first to regain himself.

"SANDBORN? What the hell…."

BLAM!

There was an instant flash of light, a deafening clap of sound, and a rushing wind that hit us like a wall of water and pushed us back down. When we looked back toward where the light and sound had come from, there was a six-foot hole where they had been standing.

"I'm sorry, Captain. I heard the ejection port lifters

spooling up, and I knew that meant someone was testing the matter/antimatter ejection system. You three were in the wrong place at the wrong time."

As we got up and began dusting ourselves off, the two men with Wilson thanked me for saving their lives and walked back to the ship. Wilson looked at me quizzically and pulled me aside. "You know, Deke, if you'd just not done anything, your whole Captain Ahriman, board of inquiry problem would have been solved. Don't think I'm not grateful. I am. Thank you for your quick action. I quite literally would be toast right now if not for you. Still, my first thought after the explosion was, 'Why would he do that?'"

"I don't know, Brice, other than it just was the right thing to do. It was what I would have wanted someone to do for me were I standing there with you. Trust me, Brice. For a split second the thought did occur to me that your death could solve a lot, but the bottom line is, I couldn't do it."

"Well, that settles it. You are a bone fide idiot, Deke." Wilson wasn't being jocular or kind. He was stating a fact and reality as he saw it. "Not only did you pass up your golden ticket, you saved the only guy on this ship who will deliver you to a board of inquiry. The icing on the cake is you might very well have died risking your life to screw all that up. I don't understand you at all, Sandborn. I thought I did, but clearly I don't."

Wilson walked away shaking his head. He was right, of course. It had been an opportunity to eliminate him, regain the captainship, avoid a board of inquiry, and skate right on by all the consequences of my actions. Before the chair, I would have done just that. I'd have heard the servos, realized what was going to happen, folded my arms, leaned up against a bulkhead, and watched the fireworks.

But since the chair.... I guess my entire outlook has changed. What happened to others matters now. I'm not responsible for what they do, but if I can help them, I should.

I followed the captain back into the ship. He was looking for whoever was at the ejector controls and, in the crew's parlance, he was going to "rip them a new one." It was Miller. I knew where he was working and I knew he would have had to test the ejectors with a quantum of matter and antimatter. Even matter and antimatter as small as a quantum would still have a relatively large reaction.

"Captain, a word?" I touched Wilson lightly on the shoulder as I caught up with him.

He whirled. "What!"

"You may want to rethink what you're about to do, sir." I tried to keep my voice as level as possible.

"Not now, Sandborn!" He turned to go again.

"Brice, it was your fault." Again my voice was level, but it brought him to a halt.

Without turning, "What was my fault?"

"The whole thing, sir. You chewed out Miller and told him in no uncertain terms to get the ejectors back on line ASAP. You took two other crews off other duty to cover his other duties so he could focus on that full time. That's all fine, sir. But then you were having a conversation with two other crew members immediately in front of the ejector ports. Ummm, immediately in front of the ports."

"Oh, crap." Wilson's shoulders slumped. It is standard protocol for any ship powered by matter/antimatter jump drives that the ports are a "no go, no stand, no step" area. It is one of the first rules they teach you in the academy and on shipboard. Standing in front of the ports isn't just a dumb thing to do, it's tantamount to grabbing a live wire or going into a reactor without protective gear. It just isn't done. Not because it's a rule (it is, of course), but because the chances are you'll die if you do it.

"Sir, you can certainly chew Miller out for not sounding an

alarm or making an announcement before the test.   He deserves that. But you shouldn't have been there in the first place.   But as captain, it is your right to give him a stern talking to. Of course, if you do chew him out, he's going to know you...ummm...were standing in front of the ports."

That pretty much put the brakes on the captain. "Sandborn, don't you have something else you could be doing?"

"Aye, Captain."

With repairs complete, we left Debris within the next 24 hours. Several weeks passed. I had done a little digging in the ship's computer after we left ISD-6709-RP and discovered the ISD designation was an acronym for InterStellar Debris. The suffix RP was clearly Rogue Planet, so the cartographer had perfectly straddled the fence by declaring good old 6709 as both debris and a rogue planet.

With the jump drives repaired and having regenerated enough antimatter to keep us moving, we were well on our way back to civilization and completing our contract. I was still more or less confined to quarters.

I asked to speak with the captain.

"What is it, Deke? I'm pretty busy."

"I can see that, Brice.   You've got enough stuff on your plate for a staff of two or three to handle, but it's pretty much just you.   That's what I wanted to talk to you about.   It occurred to me that maybe the reason you were standing in front of those ports back there on Debris was because you were and are moving too fast, doing too many things. Stuff slides when that happens."

"So?   With Ahriman dead and you confined to quarters, that pretty much leaves just me. I don't see a solution here."

"Why not use me? I'm not doing anyone any good sitting on my butt in my cabin."

"Excuse me? Use you? In case you forgot, I have relieved

you of duties pending the institution of a board of inquiry over the death of the former captain which you caused. You can't serve on this ship under that circumstance. Forget it. Bad idea."

"No, it's a good idea. In fact, I don't see you've got a lot of choice. You need help and I need something to do."

Wilson paused, looked at me, and then chuckled to himself. "Oh. OK. I get it. I let you 'help' me and you graciously take some command responsibilities off my shoulders.   Then the crew starts to see you in command again. You, being the nice guy you are, start to treat the crew with kid gloves. They respond. They prefer you. Before long, they prefer you so much that when someone says, 'We'd be better off with Sandborn as captain,' I'm out on my ear or maybe even spaced."

"Look, Brice, I don't care what you do with me. I'm telling you that even if you were to determine Captain Ahriman's death was an accident today and clear me of all charges, I do not want to take command away from you. You're doing a superb job and the crew is responding to you better than they did to Ahriman. The ship is humming."

It was as though Wilson finally heard me. He stopped. He looked me in the eye for long seconds.

"Deke, what happened to you on Debris? You have been a different person since we left. At first I didn't buy this 'new Deke', but it's been so consistent for so long, I'm beginning to think you really may be different."

"One day I'll tell you Brice, but not today. I'm still working through it all. When I get a better handle on it, I'll clue you in. But until then, I'm serious. I'm no threat to you. In fact, if you'll let me, I can be a real help to you. I've got experience, skills, and I know this ship as good as anyone.   We're jumping, but we are still limping a bit because we're being careful with the drives.   I can give them the attention you can't. And I'm already working with some crew, helping do their jobs, obviously from my quarters, giving advice, and the like. I think it is making a difference. At least there seem to be fewer 'walking dead'. Think what I could do if I could actually work with them side by side."

I was not about to tell Wilson about the chair and my experience in it. After I told Angie about the chair, he and I agreed I needed to keep the story to myself for now. I had told no one else yet. I had no plans to. If people asked, and most were so self-occupied they didn't bother to, I would just give them the "I'll tell you later" answer. "Later" might be WAY later.

We figured that if I was serious about changing; I needed to focus on just changing. After all, I had a lifetime of living one way, and suddenly now I'm living another. Better to just do it than blab about it. It was going to be an upstream swim either way. I think Angie's exact words of advice were, "No sense making it more difficult by talking crazy on top of acting crazy."

"OK, Deke, here's the deal. I'll give you run of the ship, but I want to assign you primarily to work with Chief Miller. He's a loose cannon and if you're working with him, that may settle him down a bit. When you're not working with him, you can work with whoever you please.

"I'm reducing you in rank to my old rating of 3rd mate. I'm willing to give this a try for a week or two and see how it goes. If I sense you stepping over the line even once and trying to curry favor with the crew or threatening my authority, you'll find yourself confined to quarters immediately for the duration of the trip, no questions asked. Agreed?"

"Aye, Captain."

Wilson picked up the ship's intercom and made a terse announcement to the crew about my reduction in rank and new assignment. He also made sure the crew knew this was not being done instead of the board of inquiry. I thought that was a nice touch. It more or less insured I couldn't get enough of the crew to stage a mutiny, even if I'd wanted to.

"Is that all, Captain?"

"One more thing, Deke. As a courtesy, you can keep Chief Steward Ariti for the duration of this run. Also, if you would prefer to take meals in your quarters, I would understand, but as far as I'm concerned, you are still an officer on this ship and have a right to eat in the officer's mess. I don't have to do this, but you've been straightforward with me, so I'm willing to extend this courtesy."

"Aye, Captain. Understood."

"Very well, Mr. Sandborn. You are dismissed."

I headed straight down to engineering.

It would be safe to say that Engineering Chief Miller was not at all pleased with my new assignment as his partner. The Rapacious has a decent air exchange system, but I could swear the air in the engineering spaces was blue for quite a while, following the string of curses that burst out from his mouth…and seemingly effortlessly at that. It was not your run-of-the-mill cursing that you can hear on any ship; the type that is crude. Nope. This was the genuine article, a first class tirade, with imaginative invective that seared the air like lightning released from a bottle.

I gave him a few minutes to run himself down a bit before I ventured any response.

"Feeling any better now, Chief?" I asked.

Too soon. Off he went again, with an entirely different set of curses. This guy was to cursing like Fellucci was to opera.[6]

---

[6] Apparently Fellucci was an opera singer of the late 22nd century who, as near as I could determine from Sandborn, was like Pavarotti on steroids.

He had elevated it into an art form, to be sure.

Technically, even as a 3rd Mate, I was still an officer and outranked him as an enlisted person, but that was mere formality. "Thirds" were just a tiny step above cadets in the minds of the rest of the crew. They were to be tolerated rather than obeyed. If a Third was smart, he or she would accept the guidance of the Chief they worked with and call it a learning experience.

The only thing I had going for me was I used to be First and Chief Miller knew it. He also knew that my knowledge of engineering was second only to his, so I clearly wasn't a rookie trainee. That was a problem. He didn't know what to do about me. There was no precedent. But his real problem was more difficult. In an environment that is dog eat dog, my presence threatened him.

His outburst finally subsided into something between grumbling and mumbling as he turned back to what he was doing.

"Look, Chief. I didn't ask to be assigned to work with you. That was Captain Wilson's idea. But here I am, and the last thing I want to do is get in your way and make your life more difficult. Engineering is your space. Down here you are in charge, and I can live with that. I'm not here to boss you around or micro-manage or even look over your shoulder. I'm here to work and I think I'm probably a pretty good guy to have available."

"So you say," Miller replied. "Look, Mr. Sandborn, forgive my skepticism, but I've never met anyone who got to be a First who didn't think he was too high and mighty to do the dirty work I do. I'm sorry, my Lordship, if I don't entirely trust your newfound willingness to get your hands dirty. I'm not sure what Wilson's game is, or yours for that matter, although I can't see what's in this for you at all. I am sure, though, that there is some sort of game going on here.

Nothing involving officers is ever without some sort of angle."

"I'm sorry to disappoint you, Chief. I've got nothing. I know you're a poker player, so let me put it to you in your language. You and I both have to play the hands we've been dealt. We can cooperate and it will benefit both of us, or we can argue our way to doing nothing. I'm stuck here as are you. We're going to have to work together, either the easy way or the hard way. It's your call."

Chief Miller was only slightly less stubborn than granite. Without speaking a word, he turned around and went to back to what he was doing. I could hear that mumble grumble going on under his breath.

"Well, if you're going to make yourself useful around here, check the relay coupling between the damper and the drive. I think there is some minor arcing going on in there. It may need to be rebuilt."

And that was it. We were back on track with our long haul...long in distance and in time even with a jump drive. After all there's only so much space you can bend at a time with the limited amount of energy a starship can generate. There was also the whole issue of having to avoid using the jump drive when there were other "masses" within the boundaries of the space and time we were seeking to bend. Bending space with them in it would ruin their day, and potentially could enlarge the temporary mini black hole we were creating by sucking them in. The increase in mass would enlarge the hole and suck us in, too.

Work with Miller began and continued for days upon end. Engineering handles the upkeep of every single mechanical and electrical device on the ship from the jump drives down to the servo switch that turns the light on when a crew person opens the slider on his or her closet. There is always something to fix. Always.

It took about a week before Miller stopped checking my work after I finished every job. I suppose it was only partly to do with demonstrating who was in charge. After all, he needed to make sure I knew what I was doing and did it right.

It took another week before he'd let me work apart from him. Once he didn't feel the need to micro-manage me, my value to him increased if I could be tasked with repairs in one place while he worked in another.

By the third week, he was actually comfortable working with me on a project. We tackled a major refit in the antimatter generators...a three-man job, really...but we managed to get it done by ourselves. We not only replaced some worn parts, we also noodled a modification to the electron routing panel that was not in the original design, but it increased antimatter production by almost a third. Neither of us would have seen it individually, but together it became obvious.

The truth is that once I got to know Miller, I liked him. He was gruff, opinionated, and headstrong; but he was honest and capable. And while I wouldn't call him a comedian, his command of swear words and his sense of timing in using them cracked me up on more than one occasion.

I don't know that Miller ever liked me. He didn't dislike me. It's just that "liking" wasn't a common trait shown between crew members. He did grow to respect me and I think he grudgingly thought I wasn't a complete idiot, engineering-wise.

My relationship with Angie grew over these weeks and our discussions continued as often as we both had time. Slowly he saw the reality of my emerging evolution. As a man who spent his career serving others, he only ever saw the service he gave, not the "others". His service was a product or duty. Service was what he did. His focus was on being good at it, perfecting it, refining it.

However, he never actually saw the people he was serving. His viewpoint stopped with the service. The person was irrelevant, unimportant. And so his service, while excellent, was cold and without feeling.

From my perspective, I was, piece by piece, rebuilding the end of every life I had lived in the chair. While the scenarios onboard the Rapacious were nothing like the death scenes of the chair, I knew each person I was helping was a brick I was cementing in place for a changed life…a meaningful life. How could I have missed this all these years? How could something so incredibly important have escaped my understanding?

From my perspective, I was just helping people, but Angie saw what I was doing with Miller and the others as service, similar to what he did. That began to change, though. At first, he thought we were doing the same thing, and in a way, we were. Then, however, he began to see a difference. The object of my "helping" was the person I was helping. The object of his "serving" was always and only the service itself. He saw that my serving was to help the individual, to make the individual's life better or easier. His service was for himself, to keep his job and advance if possible. It was like mine in form, but the objectives were totally different.

Service of any kind, he began to realize, wasn't complete in and of itself. It was the means to an end. He saw that his service could be a tool rather than a product; that serving others could be something that enabled change in the person being served. Simultaneously he began to understand that the benefit of that to him would be meaning, that what he did would have meaning. A loop was created. Service created change for others that returned to the server as a sense of meaning and purpose.

What I had learned by virtue of infinite deaths and

eternities of loneliness in the chair, he began to learn by observing my example. I didn't intend to be an example. I was just walking out my personal oath to change. Somehow that very personal commitment to live a life of connection and service radiated in a way that others might see and understand even just as observers.

The weeks blended into one another. I think I got to work with all the crew, even the mess rats at one time or another. Like each crew member I worked with, I was focused on getting the work done. Unlike any crew member, I could have cared less to get the credit...a fact that was not lost on anyone.

I was actually enjoying the work itself. In some ways, the more menial the better. Menial work was unwanted work. Everyone was looking to move up. So if I helped the crew on the bottommost rungs, and let them take the credit, they were the most appreciative.

Life was good. In fact, it was very good.

Until the day we docked in the spaceport and the squad of police showed up, placed me under arrest and led me off the ship in handcuffs.

CHAPTER 10 - **Trial by Fire**

Wilson was wrong. It wasn't a maritime matter. It had become a civilian criminal matter and the local constabulary was holding me on murder charges. This would not be a board of maritime officers looking into the situation. This was going to be a criminal investigation followed by a trial, and if I was found guilty, some sort of punishment up to and including execution. I had expected the maritime service would have conducted a board of inquiry, which would have found there were no grounds for criminal prosecution. That would have been the end of it.

Somewhere along the line, though, the civilian authorities at the port had decided to press murder charges. Once criminal charges are pressed, according to Admiralty Law, which held in space as on the seas of Earth, that eliminated the need for a board of inquiry. I was going to be tried for murder.

The police who physically arrested me were actually

Coasties,[7] and in short order they had turned me over to the local police authority.[8] I was languishing in a cell at the moment.

"Deacon Sandborn?"

"Yes. That's me."

"Good. My name is Cogley, Samuel T. Cogley. I'm your court-appointed attorney. Got a minute?" He paused and smiled. "I'm sorry. I couldn't resist. I don't get to use that line very often, so I like to take advantage of every chance I get."

"Apology accepted Lawyer Cogley," I said. "I'm glad to have a little humor. There has been little of it today."

Samuel T. Cogley was exactly what you'd expect from a lawyer out here in the space boonies. He was a small man, maybe a bit shorter than Angie, wiry, with a prematurely receding hairline that made his head look too big for his body.

---

[7] Sandborn continued to correct my error prone expectations of the future. Just like the maritime services had been the real force expanding space exploration and not the military, so it was with law enforcement in space. As on the seas of Earth where it was each country's local "coast guard" that had the authority to regulate both commercial and personal craft on the water, so it was in space. The maritime organizations on Earth had worked hand in hand with their local "Coasties" over the years, so it was to be expected those Guardsmen would provide the same policing in space as they did on the seas. Their official title was The United Space Guard, but everyone called them by their Earth moniker. Only they had the authority to board the Rapacious and take Sandborn into custody.

[8] Except for newer outposts and strictly scientific installations, every planet that was inhabited/colonized had declared themselves "Ports of Authority". This was an extension of the Port Authority concept from Earth where the local Port Authority took over from where the Coast Guard left off. Since most colonized planets tended to have the majority of their populations located around space ports, this was all the policing authority that was needed. The Coasties had turned Sandborn over to the local Port Authority Police.

But there was this energy that sort of emanated from him. Maybe it was the way he was continually standing on the balls of his feet, as though he were getting ready to run a sprint. Or it could have been his watery blue eyes that stood in stark contrast to his olive skin and brown hair. When he spoke, you got the impression he had already thought first. His manner was crisp and intentional.

"Please, call me Sam. I've read the file on this, what little there is in it, and I'm hoping you can fill me in on all the missing pieces."

"You can call me Deke, Sam. Where would you like me to start?"

"Why don't you start with a synopsis of the events leading up to the day of the captain's death and then give me as complete a recounting of what happened that day. I'm going to take some notes."

That took me by surprise. Most handwriting had gone the way of the polar bears and things were done by transcribers...small hand held solid state mini recording computers. Apparently Lawyer Cogley was not just "old school"; he was "ancient school".

It took a little over an hour to relate the story to him. He did not interrupt me once, but wrote continuously and, at times, furiously while I spoke. When I finished, I fell silent, waiting for him to speak. He spent a few minutes finishing his note taking, set his pencil down (at least I think that's what it was...I'd never actually seen one), and looked up toward the ceiling.

"Who was the first person into the area after the altercation?"

"I don't really know, Sam. I had passed out from the blow to the back of my head and when I came to, I was already in the infirmary. I never thought to ask who found me."

"Hmmm. I'll have to interview the crew. Any guesses so I

can start with someone who might know?"

"I'd start with Chief Miller. I was in engineering when it happened and that's his bailiwick. Failing that, I'd talk with Captain Wilson. In fact, protocol suggests that you start with him instead of Miller. That way you'll have his permission to talk with whoever you need to."

Cogley took some additional notes, put his gear away, and took his leave. It was good to have someone to talk to about it. And it was good to have a lawyer who at least seemed to know what he was doing. But I still had no idea what was going to happen and what my chances of getting off were. I was sure it was self-defense and that nothing should happen to me, but that was just me. There were no witnesses, and it is possible the pattern of injuries could be interpreted multiple ways.

A day later: "Deke, it's me, Sam. Got a minute? Oh. Wait. I already used that one."

Grinning, I greeted him back. This time the officer accompanied him and opened my cell door to allow him to come in.

"Deke, we've got a problem."

That was the last thing I wanted to hear from my lawyer. "What? A problem with the evidence? How bad is it?"

"Oh, no. The evidence is clear as a bell. After hearing your story and inspecting the area where it happened, I'm convinced and I think a jury would be, too. Your wound is clearly from behind and his wounds are totally consistent with your story. So unless what really happened was that you planned to sneak up on him from the front, in a crouch, and decided to hit him with the top of your head on his chin from below, and then you turned your back on him so he could whack you on the back of the head with a wrench, and then you turned around again and pushed him against the wall with deadly force...you're in good shape.

"No, the problem is different and potentially bigger. Did you know that Ahriman's father is in the merchant marine? And did you know he is the commandant of this sector? And his command is based at this port?"

"No."

I meant "no" not in the short, clipped sense of "no, I didn't know," but rather in the long, drawn out sense of "no, it can't be true."

"Yes. And Draven Ahriman wants an eye for an eye."

Time passed fairly quickly even though I was locked up. There wasn't much for the local authorities to investigate once they interviewed the crew, took my statement, and viewed the scene. It had been so long since the actual fight that the physical evidence, such as there was, was compromised long ago. It took a little over two days to process it all.

There was no point in stringing anything out but the authorities did have to give my lawyer a chance to prepare his case, so they scheduled the trial for the beginning of the following week. Sam Cogley was an almost daily bright spot to my day. Despite Commandant Ahriman's insertion of himself in the investigation and prosecution, Sam continued to be convinced that they would drop murder charges, and that there was not even enough evidence to justify an involuntary manslaughter charge.

"It was self-defense, Deke. He struck first, from a blind side, without warning. You were protecting yourself from further harm. There was no intent, no malice, no motivation present beyond just getting him away from you. This is going to be a walk in the park."

"Can Commodore Ahriman affect the outcome in any way?"

"He can try. He might dig up character witnesses against you. He can cast doubt as to whether you have as clean hands as you say. He might even try to influence the case to suggest you were waiting for an opportunity to kill his son to take over his position. If he does it right, he could create substantial doubt about your innocence. But the judge will instruct the jury they cannot convict you based on suspicion and poor character. There has to be tangible proof that convinces them you did it beyond any reasonable doubt. You may be the baddest guy ever, but even if you did it on purpose, the evidence to convict just isn't there.

"No, I suspect your real problem with Ahriman is going to be after the trial."

"What do you mean?" I asked.

Sam looked me square in the eye. "He will not try to destroy you at the trial in order to get a conviction. He knows there's not enough evidence to convict you. I heard the prosecutor wanted to drop the case, but Ahriman intervened and put pressure on him through the Port Authority to continue. No, Ahriman wants to destroy you at the trial so he can hold all of that against you after you walk free.

"After the trial, did you think you were just going to go back on the Rapacious and be Wilson's second in command? If you don't go back to the Rapacious, do you think with this on your record and Ahriman's authority and pull that any other maritime crew would accept you?

"No, son. As long as you are in the maritime service, Commodore Ahriman is going to make your life a living hell. He's going to see to it that you never get an officer's billet ever again. He's going to see to it that you only get posted on the worst vessels under the worst captains. And he's going to insure personally that every captain knows that they will earn his eternal gratitude by making your life on board as absolutely miserable as possible.

"As long as you are in the maritime service, he will own

you."

It was so obvious I should have seen it. I had, without trying, created the worst possible enemy in my chosen profession. My future was ruined...torn to shreds. I would be a marked man in the service. The truth hit like a thunderbolt. My life as a maritime officer was over, regardless of the outcome of this trial.

The trial went exactly as Sam predicted. The prosecution was half-hearted because they knew they had no case. They were going through the motions to satisfy Ahriman. True to Sam's prediction, Ahriman produced both live testimony and vids of former coworkers who had nothing good to say about me at all. Their accusations were salacious and beyond anything I had actually done. But when your ultimate commanding officer tells you what he wants you to say beforehand, you say what you think he wants to hear. I'm sure each of those men received something of value in return for their testimony...like a promotion or advantageous transfer.

In the end, the jury acquitted me. I was a free man, at least in the eyes of the law.

Ahriman was there on the last day. I could tell he didn't expect any different outcome, but he approached me as the court was dismissed.

"Congratulations, Sandborn. They found you innocent, and the trial is over. Enjoy this feeling of freedom. It will not last long."

I was in uniform. Sam thought it wouldn't hurt to advertise that I was a professional seaman and an officer. He wanted to leave the impression with the jury like the whole "officer and a gentleman" riff. Ahriman was resplendent in his uniform as well.

Normally maritime officers do not salute indoors, but I felt this was worth a small breech of protocol. I replaced my cap, came to attention, and snapped a perfect salute.

"Commodore, with respect, sir, I tender my resignation as an officer in the maritime service, effective immediately. Now if the Commodore will excuse me, I have a life to get on with."

I executed a second salute, did a perfect parade ground about face, and walked briskly out of the court and into the fresh air. If Ahriman said anything or had any reaction, I did not see it. Nor did I care.

The last part about having "a life to get on with" was bravado on my part. I had no clue what I was going to do. Because I resigned rather than being discharged, I had back pay, some cash benefits, and a ton of unused paid vacation I would get paid for. In addition, I'd put away quite a bit of money in a retirement fund which, for a penalty, I could get my hands on. There were also some investments I had made with the money left to me when the last of my parents died. I wasn't going to starve. But what was I going to do?

I met with Sam the next day and he had a bunch of paperwork I had to sign in order for the verdict to be entered into my records and so he could get paid by the court. In the short time I'd known him, he'd become a friend of sorts, so I asked him.

"Sam, now that I've resigned my commission, do you have any suggestions what I might do to earn a living?"

"Most of my cases involve the maritime service in one way or another. I'm not sure how you got to be the rank you were before you killed Ahriman, but from what I can tell you are a poor fit with a service that prides itself on the ambition and aggression of its officers. I think you're well rid of it.

"Now as to what you might do, it seems to me the only thing you are truly fit for by education, training, and experience is space-faring. You should go independent. You've got the head for it. And to tell you the truth, the record you now have, being accused of murder and all, well, that fits pretty well with the aura of an independent space freight operator." Sam winked.

"I suppose you're right, Sam. It is the most logical thing, even if the general population thinks it's only an itty bitty step above a pirate."

"Of course I'm right, son. When you get your own cargo ship, and you will, stop by my office and I'll help you work through the registration paperwork, on the house. We don't get many murder trials here, so there isn't much call for criminal lawyers. I keep body and soul together by doing contract law, wills, and the like. I enjoyed this little break from my usual monotony of red tape and paperwork."

I bid Sam Cogley good-by and he turned back to his work as I left his office.

I had a couple of stops I needed to make before I commenced this new life. First, I had to go find a room for a couple of nights. Now that I had resigned my commission, I could no longer stay on the ship. Second, I needed to go to the ship and gather my belongings and take them to whatever room I would find. Finally, I needed to go back to the jail and pick up the scant possessions I had left there. And then? Well, we'd cross that bridge when we got to it.

Finding a room was no big deal, but finding a room that the innkeeper would let me sign for without a deposit (my money was at the Rapacious) was a little more difficult. The third place agreed to hold a room for me for three hours, but no more.

So I went to the Rapacious next. I had a strong suspicion my reception would be anything but welcoming. There was no doubt in my mind that Commodore Ahriman would have already communicated with Captain Wilson. His rank alone would have made an impression on a brand new captain. There was also no doubt that Ahriman would have made it crystal clear to Wilson how he wanted me treated.

I feared the worst. It turned out to be worse than that.

CHAPTER 11 - **Revenant**

The reward for Wilson's cooperation in my humiliation I learned later was the confirmation of him as the Master of the Vessel Rapacious. His captainship in hand, to say he was curt with me would have been kind. I arrived to find my quarters ransacked and most of my personal items besides my clothes either gone or in pieces.

The word had gotten out to the crew I was no longer in the service, that I had quit in disgrace, and that my property was therefore forfeit. There is no such tradition or protocol in the maritime service, but that didn't seem to matter. Wilson turned a blind eye to it all.

After inspecting my cabin and pulling together what I could, I made my way to the officer's mess to find Captain Wilson. A growing number of crew began to collect and follow me as I made my way through the ship. There was quite a crowd as I entered the mess.

"Captain, although you no doubt already know it, I have tendered my resignation to Commodore Ahriman effective immediately. As of midnight tonight I will surrender my identification, insignia, and all materials belonging to the maritime service or the Rapacious. I am giving you notice, as per regulations, that I am leaving the ship and will not be returning. I request my duties be assigned immediately to someone else. With your permission, sir!"

With that I came to attention and saluted the Captain. I held the salute, waiting for his in return. It slowly became apparent that he would not return my salute, a final evidence of the disdain he accorded me. I slowly lowered my hand.

Without looking up he simply said, "You are relieved, Mr. Sandborn. The sooner you leave the ship, the better. You are no longer welcome aboard this vessel. Nor do I expect you are welcome on any vessel of the maritime service. Tradition says I should wish a departing officer fair winds and following seas, but to you, I do not. In fact, I wish you the opposite. Get off my ship!"

Despite the lack of courtesy, I saluted again, pivoted, and walked purposefully out of the mess. I collected my bags at my quarters, and within moments I was off the ship. I did not look back.

I went to the boarding house, had dinner, listened to the conversation in the common room, and went to bed.

The next morning I walked into Sam Cogley's office. "Hey, Sam. Got a minute?"

He looked up and smiled. "Nice. Use an old man's joke on him." He chuckled, took off his glasses and stood up. "I didn't think I'd see you for a couple of days. What brings you here?"

"Well, Sam, I'm in the market for a ship and it occurred to me that most ships of the age and price I'm looking for are probably ones some of your clients may have exercised a lien on. What can you tell me."

"I can't tell you much, Deke. There aren't a lot of ships this far out. We're not at the complete end of the civilized universe but I believe you could throw a stick and hit it from here. So without a lot of traffic, there aren't a lot of ships to pick over.

"But on the other hand, there aren't a lot of guys like you looking to break into the independent cargo business, so given you're here, and given you're apparently buying, that makes you a major market force…you know, a big fish in a small pond."

It was true enough. Sam was referring to the cycle of used ships. The large cargo carriers essentially commissioned all their ships from ship builders. They almost universally bought new. The smaller ships were considered "local" as opposed to "long haul" and were often found at the end of various routes in large ports that served as hubs for distribution to smaller ports in that region.

"Sam, I know there isn't going to be anything from the larger carriers out here. I'm figuring this far out there just may be some ships that are either abandoned, or more likely owned by small shippers that had a lien on a guy's independent operation that went belly up and they took his ship in payment. I figured in the event that happened, there'd be paperwork. And if there was paperwork, you might be the guy to do it. Any of those laying around?"

"Well, let me think." He rubbed his chin a bit and gazed into space. "There are a couple that come to mind. But, Deke, why come to me? You could have asked around at the space port and actually seen the ships.

"Oh, wait a minute. I know why. You don't have any money!"

"Actually I do, but other than my muster out pay, it is all tied up in investments back on Earth and it would take months to get it here to use to buy something. I don't have that kind of time."

"So you want me to work a deal for you. It's less about the ship and more about working a deal to buy it without ready money. Well, it just so happens you have come to the right place. Deke, I've got a small-time shipper who has just the ship you're looking for. It is a short haul 'local' and it was on its third owner. That guy lost his shirt on a run that cost him an arm and a leg. His jump drive failed him and he had to limp home on sub-luminal drives. It took him months and his crew costs killed him, not to mention the necessary repairs to the jump drive which he couldn't afford to do.

"The guy that owns it is sitting on it. He doesn't want it... at least he doesn't want the trouble of running it. He wants to sell it, but no one is buying. Who'd want a tub with jump drive issues. At least that's the perception in the marketplace. I know for a fact the jump drives are repairable, but anyone who might otherwise be interested is concerned it is junk because of that. Are you interested?"

"I might be. The jump drives don't concern me. I can repair them in my sleep. It is the 'nut', the money I'd have to put down on the ship to get it. Ideally, I'd like to give the guy a really small percentage of the value of the ship and have him continue to hold the paper. I'd commit to making runs and giving him 50% of the profit from each run until I pay the note off. That way I could essentially buy the ship a run at a time. Does that make sense?"

"Yes, Deke, it does," said Sam. "But I don't know if it will to my guy. He just wants to get rid of it for whatever he can get. What may sweeten the pot is if you offer to run his cargo for just crew costs and operational overhead. If he were to get in essence cut rate shipping for his own cargo as well as a piece of the profit on anyone else's cargo you picked up along the way, he might go for it."

We knocked the idea around for another few minutes and shaped it into what I thought was a pretty attractive package. Then Sam picked up the vid-phone and gave his client a call.

It took some doing, but he went for it.

Sam, true to his word, took care of the paperwork gratis. The down payment was roughly equal to my mustering out pay, which I got later that afternoon and took to Sam.

"I just need one more thing to complete the paperwork. I assume you're going to rename her...unless you like the current name."

"Which is what?" I asked.

"CS Plunger," said Sam.

"Change it!"

"Thought so, but to what?" Sam asked.

"CS Revenant."

Sam looked up. "That's appropriate, I guess, given the outcome of your court case."

"It's appropriate for many more reasons than that."

So I named her Revenant. As Sam said, it seemed appropriate.

It took a couple of days for Sam Cogley to get the paperwork done to get the Revenant licensed. He was true to his word, and his services did not cost me a cent.

The Revenant was a smaller cargo cruiser, about a third to half the size of the Rapacious. It needed a crew of at least three, five would have been better, and seven ideal. I presently had a crew of one: me. But you can't get a crew together without first having a ship, so I had to take the leap and buy this one to get the ball rolling.

In the meantime, I spent every waking hour working on the Revenant. My first visit was with high hopes that it was possibly flight ready and I might fire up at least the maneuvering engines and take it aloft for an evaluation spin. My hopes did not survive my first view of the craft.

It was in sorry shape. Even from the outside, it was clear it had been used and abused. The inside was worse. The maintenance logs were a mess. It appeared even basic maintenance hadn't been done. There were literally no entries for the last three years of operations. That would mean virtually every system on the ship would need some work done on it. The jump drives would be the most difficult and complex. They should have been overhauled at least once during the period. No wonder there were problems there.

Life support, navigation, helm, hull integrity, communications, non-flight engineering, and flight engineering would all need to at least be checked at a minimum. I could do it. I was certainly trained and qualified. The time it would take to do it right was another matter. It would take a crew of five at least a week of 16-hour days to accomplish just the routine "tear downs" and inspections. Then any actual repairs and/or replacement of worn parts would be time and cost on top of that. That might require another several days added in, assuming all the parts were readily available, and I could afford them. And you couldn't assume that.

There just being me, the time multiplied beyond my capacity.

Still, just being me, I had no choice. If it was going to get done at all, I was going to have to do it. So I started right then and there on a tear down of the sub-light engines. Almost immediately I saw nearly a half dozen capacitors burned to a crisp. This ship must have limped into port and when it set down, the crew knew it was not going to lift off again. That might explain why they didn't bother to fight the repossession. It also might explain why I got such a favorable deal from the cargo shipper that repossessed it.

I made a list of several other things I would need and went to see the yard supervisor. The yard served not only as a storage for out of service ships, but also as a junkyard for harvesting parts. I found the yard supervisor in his office.

"Excuse me, my name is Sandborn and I'm the new owner of the cargo cruiser you have. You may have seen me working on it. I have a list of parts I need for some maintenance I'm trying to complete. Can you help me?"

"I know who you are, Mr. Sandborn. Gimme your list." His manner was abrupt, bordering on rude. With a scowl he barely read through it.

"I'm sorry, Mr. Sandborn. I have nothing on this list available for you."

"Excuse me? You have three other derelicts of the same make and model of my ship in your parts inventory. You have duplicates and maybe even triplicates of these things."

"No, Mr. Sandborn, I don't. Oh, I have the parts; no doubt about that. It's just that they are not for sale...to you."

"Why? If you've got them, why can't you sell them?"

"That's because they're already sold. So I can't sell them to you."

"I don't understand. Who would buy three ships' worth of parts?"

"The Maritime Services requisitioned these parts not a day and a half ago. I'm under contract with them and once they requisition a part, no matter how long it takes for them to get around to using it, it belongs to them."

"I don't believe you."

"Here's the requisition request, signed by the Commodore himself."

The light dawned. The paperwork for the Revenant not only had to be filed with the local port authority, but also the Maritime Services would get the paperwork should the new owner want to hire a crew provided by the Services. Ahriman. He just wasn't going to give up. He was going to try and stop me any way he could.

"Yup. Everything appears to be in order here. Sorry to bother you."

I took my leave and headed straight to Sam Cogley's office. I was hot, red hot. There had to be a way around this.

"Can he do this, Sam? Can he just buy up everything I need to keep me from getting it?"

"'Fraid so, Deke. Out here, his authority is almost absolute concerning large cargo shipping. While the size of ship you're going to operate isn't normally subject to his authority, he has the ability to make life difficult for anyone who doesn't want to cooperate with him to get at you."

"OK, I get that. What he can, he orders done. What he can't, he threatens others to get done. Is there no solution here? Because if I can't get those parts, The Revenant isn't going to ever get off the ground."

"Hmmm," mused Sam. "Sometimes, where a frontal assault fails, an attack at the flanks will succeed. I have an idea."

Chapter 12 - **First Crew**

I didn't know whether Sam's idea was valid or not, but I really didn't have a choice. So I concentrated on what I could do.

Shipping smaller cargos on longer runs to yield higher profits is a delicate balance between size of the cargo and distance to be traveled. Even with a smaller ship, the longer the distance, the greater the freight charges. That's good, right? Well, yes, as long as you can afford the operating expenses and crew salaries and still make a profit on the run. The longer the run, the higher both costs were. So there was a point of diminishing returns where you couldn't carry enough cargo to cover the costs for an excessively long run.

To get around that, you could "stack the deck" in your favor by carrying more valuable cargo. More valuable meant cargo that it had a greater value when sold and distributed. The owner of those goods would be willing to pay more for their delivery.

More valuable might mean riskier cargo. Often there was cargo that the maritime service just would not handle because of various risks, like explosion. Independents would handle those and could charge a premium for the inherent riskiness of the cargo.

In either of those situations, you could contract to go longer distances because there was enough margin in the freight charges to make it all work.

It sounds good, but that's where a lot of my predecessors ended up losing their shirts or their lives. Sometimes things blew up financially. Sometimes they blew up literally.

I knew I was going to have to engage in a few of those types of runs to make ends meet, but hey, that's the business.

Now that I had a ship that was costing me money (maintenance, docking fees, provisioning, etc.), besides repairs, I had two other problems I had to solve immediately. I needed a contract to move freight, and I needed a crew of at least two more than myself. Sam had some local contacts, and he was able to put in a good word for me, so coming up with a contract wasn't that difficult. I had a signed one for a short haul run to a nearby colony, taking some raw materials to them and bringing some finished goods back. One problem down.

The second problem resolved itself in a most unexpected way. Two days later, there was a knock on the door of my rented room in the evening. I wasn't expecting anyone.

"Who's there?" I asked without bothering to get up from what I was doing.

"Angie. Angie Ariti. Is that you, Mr. Sandborn?"

"Angie? Hold on a minute. I'm coming."

Angie would be the first crew from the Rapacious that I had seen since I resigned. I assumed that Wilson's cargo contractors had given him instructions for another run, and The Rapacious had buttoned up and departed by now.

"Hi, Mr. Sandborn. Do you have some time? Do you mind if I come in?"

"Of course, Angie. I've got time and please come in. I'm surprised to see you. I thought the Rapacious had sailed, and you'd be long gone on another run."

"Oh, it sailed, sir. It left this morning on another long haul, this one heading toward Earth."

"I don't understand, Angie. If it sailed, why are you still here?"

"That's a great question, Mr. Sandborn. I thought I would be on board... until this morning at least. As we were making preparations to get underway, I suddenly realized I didn't want to go. No, that's not really it. I realized I no longer fit there. I've never felt that way in my life. You must forgive me, Mr. Sandborn. I haven't talked to anyone about this until now, and I'm struggling to find the right words to fit."

Angie paused. "Let me try again. When I say I felt like I didn't fit any longer, it sounds like I'm saying I felt like I fit before that. I'm not. I don't know that I ever felt like I fit anywhere before, or didn't fit. It wasn't something I ever spent any time thinking about. If I had, I would have thought it was stupid to think about such things, and pushed it away. But this morning, I woke up realizing I didn't fit; I didn't belong...and it mattered. It mattered a lot, in fact. It mattered enough for me to walk into Mr. Wilson's quarters and resign, right then and there."

I was stunned. Oh, I could see Angie changing ships. That kind of thing happened all the time. Sometimes you tired of the same ship and the same runs and the same shipmates, and change was a good thing. You left one ship and found another.

This was different. He'd resigned. He didn't just leave the Rapacious. He left the service.

I gave a low whistle. "Angie, this is a big deal. Tell me what's going on."

After I returned to the ship from my "eternities" in the chair, Angie and I had spent some very significant time talking about the meaning and ramifications of such a thing. We had some deep discussions. Really deep discussions. So it didn't strike me as peculiar that after quitting his career, he might seek me out to talk about it. So I encouraged him.

"Mr. Sandborn, I didn't sit in the chair. You did. But by the time we'd reached port, I think I felt as close as possible what sitting in the chair might actually feel like. I can't say it has changed me like it changed you, but I can say that it started me questioning what I do, and how and why I do it.

"Actually, you did that, Mr. Sandborn. How you acted after the chair affected me more than what you told me about the chair. I watched you working with the other members of the crew, Miller especially, when you didn't have to.

"I watched you work with Miller when he didn't want to have anything to do with you. Shoot, he didn't want to have anything to do with anybody. But if he wouldn't let you work with him, you worked beside him. And you worked for him. And then, after he finally realized there was really nothing in it for you, he let you work with him.

"I watched you pick guys up who were the walking dead, and by the time you were halfway through whatever they were working on, you made them different. Guys that for years just did the minimum to get by, I saw slowly but surely begin to get some pride in what they were doing. And I saw that pride begin to grow as they became more and more self sufficient. That was you, sir. That was your demeanor, your attitude, and your passion. It changed them.

"Then I saw you working with the party crowd, the guys who'd get anyone and everyone to do their work for them while they got high or drunk or, well, other things. At first they just used you as a handy slave. But you did the work and asked for more and actually looked like you enjoyed what you were doing. They noticed. Then they looked more closely. Then they stopped partying and joined in, working with you side by side. And when you left to move on to the next job, they didn't go back to partying. It was like they had found something...a purpose maybe...but something that changed them.

"I saw stuff get done on that ship I've never seen get done on any other ship I've ever been on. You were like a virus...a really good virus...but you infected these guys with a sense of purpose and worth.

"You know what made it work? You wanted to help them. You wanted to. That never happened, ever. And it got to them. If you, being the #2 guy on the ship, actually wanted to help them do the jobs they do day in and day out, that meant you saw what they did as important. And it wasn't too great a leap for them to feel that you thought them important, too. Do you know how infectious that is? It's like you uncovered some sort of hidden desire they had all along that they didn't know they had: the desire to be appreciated and valued.

"I saw all this. I saw how subtle it was, but how great the impact was. You weren't trying to change anyone. You were just doing what you thought was the right thing to do. Maybe that's part of what made it so powerful...that you had no motivation other than to just help.

"Then the pieces began to click into place for me. You focused on them, not the job. The job was just a means of helping them...it was them, the crew you wanted to help. You couldn't have cared less if the job was adjusting the jump drives or cleaning latrines. If it was important to them, you made it important to you.

"This morning I remembered that old discussion we had about me focusing on my service to others, but you focusing on the others whom you were serving. I've given excellent service all my life, but I realized for all that, I've changed no one. You did without hardly trying.

"So I resigned this morning because I could not just go back to the way things were. If I tried, it would have been hollow and pointless. I guess I never realized until now how selfish my life really was. I was serving, sure. But I was doing it for my sake, for my benefit. Yet, there really was no benefit to be had. In the end, it would all count for nothing.

"Looking at you working with those men, I saw beyond the pale shadow of my own way of life. I saw a reality that I didn't know existed. Now that I've seen it, how can I just go back to the old way?

"Mr. Sandborn, I don't know what to do next. I just know what I can't do any longer. So, I came to you.

"You asked me one time in all my years of being a mess rat, was there ever someone who I thought worth following. At the moment you asked that, my first thought was no, and I told you so. But as the days went by and I watched the consistency of your dealings with the crew, I realized that my first answer was no longer true. You, Mr. Sandborn, are a man worth following.

"So here I am. Got any work for me to do?"

I sat quietly, still stunned, but for a wholly different reason. My natural intention is to push such compliments away. I inherently don't trust them. However, there was a growing realization I was being offered a gift and to deny it would be to forfeit it…and I was not going to do that.

"As a matter of fact, Angie, I do. Want to be a pirate?"

I laid out the whole of the recent events leading up to the purchase of the Revenant and the new contract, the plan to run independent cargo services, the risk, the potential, the entire spectrum of possibilities. I asked him if he wanted to crew with me.

Angie fixed his gaze on me. "Sign on as what?"

"It's too small a ship for anything but crew, Angie. There's no officer versus enlisted. Heck, there's not even going to be any departments. As a crew, we are all going to have to lend a hand doing everything. I suppose I'll be a captain, but that's just because I own it. I think you know me well enough now to know that means nothing. I need crew that will work together to get the job done. Does that answer your question?"

"It does, sir. I expected, knowing you, that would be the way it would be. I'm not sure I totally can see how it is going to work, but I suspect we'll sort of figure it out as we go along. So am I in?"

"Perhaps. Angie, you know I don't need a steward on my crew."

"I know, Mr. Sandborn. I'm a qualified first class navigator in the service. I think that's a transferable skill you can use. I can also do some piloting, but I'm a better navigator."

"I figured you had some training outside of the crew mess what with the service's insistence that everyone on a space craft has to know duties other than their own in case of emergencies. The last thing anyone needs in an emergency is a mess rat. Navigation, huh? Yup, that's definitely a plus."

"So I'm in?"

"Not so fast, Angie. There is one thing you have to agree to before I can let you in. It's non-negotiable."

"What's that, Mr. Sandborn?"

"You have to call me Deke," I said.

"Aye, sir. Deke it is."

I'll bet my smile was a parsec wide. Having Angie sign on as my first crew member was almost beyond hope. And having his as a fully trained and qualified space navigator was the icing on the cake. This might actually work.

"Angie, have you found a place to stay?"

"Not yet, Mr....uh, Deke. I didn't really know what plans

to make until I'd talked to you."

"OK. Head over to the Revenant. There's crew quarters aboard. Pick a space for yourself. No sense in renting something. See if you can get in without the yard supervisor noticing. That's important. I'll be by in the morning and we'll figure out next steps. We'll be on our way as soon as I can get at least one more crew member and complete repairs."

As though on cue, there was a loud, insistent pounding on my door.

I swung open the door and there, large as life, stood Chief Engineer Burkhardt Miller, his right hand drawn back ready to repeat the staccato rapping on my door.

"Miller? What the…".

"Mr. Sandborn. I'm glad to find you in. Ariti? What are you doing here?" Miller's gaze took in my room and could not fail to see Angie standing there.

"Miller. Nice to see you, too." Angie by now had a bit of a twinkle going in his eyes. He was Greek, I think, but he sure looked downright Irish from time to time. "I might well ask you the same question, Bucko."

"Mr. Ariti has left the service and has joined on as a crew member of my new ship, the Revenant. It appears, also, he shares my curiosity of what brings you to my door tonight."

And so began the second strange conversation of the night. Like Angie, Bucky had resigned and left the Rapacious and the service behind. Unlike Angie, his reason was far more personal.

Bucky Miller was dying.

CHAPTER 13 - **First Run**

Bucky described his condition as a rare form of genetic abnormality that caused his cranial blood vessels to develop aneurysms. He'd had minor strokes on two occasions when small aneurysms burst. Fortunately for him, they were small, and he was in civilization when it happened. Prompt treatment is critical to avoid death. And even when death wasn't the outcome, without fast treatment, life-long neurological defects could occur.

As Miller got older, his aneurysms got larger. At first he would regularly submit himself to surgery to have the larger ones "coiled" to prevent them from bursting. However, the rate of development was high enough the doctors could not keep up with the new occurrences. At some point, he realized the handwriting was on the wall. It was only a matter of time before a burst was too large to repair, or couldn't be repaired quick enough. Bucky decided to live what life was left to him.

"Mr. Sandborn, when you resigned something snapped inside of me. I had hoped you would come back on board and maybe even be captain. Working with you after leaving Debris changed me somehow. I don't know if I can put it into words because I'm not a word kind of guy. It just felt like I'd been asleep all my life, and when I began to trust you were who you said you were, I woke up.

"Without realizing it, I'd been marking time the way I was living. Subconsciously, I was just waiting for one of those giant aneurysms to burst. Every day was like the previous one, all meaningless.

"But then I saw something in you I had never seen before. I don't have a word for it. You just seemed to have a reason for living...maybe a purpose. When I compared your life to mine, well, there was no comparison. My life was nothing compared to yours.

"I'm sure that hit a lot of guys who took the time to notice on the ship, but for me, knowing any day could be my last one, it took on a huge meaning. I found myself laying in my rack at night thinking that if I had one more day to live or ten or a hundred or even a thousand, what did it matter if they didn't count for something.

"So when you resigned and left the ship, it was a no brainer. I wanted to learn your secret, sir."

Once again I was filled with that sense of being given a gift and was even more conscious of needing to be careful not to reject it.

"I understand, Miller. And I am moved by the hope you are placing in me. I will do the best I can to help you know it."

Between Angie and me, we filled Bucky in on our current situation and he was quick to volunteer to join the crew. I was both pleased and relieved to have someone who was to engines like I believe Angie would be to people.

"But how are we going to get the parts we need to do the repairs now that Commodore Ahriman has them all locked up?" Clearly Miller was still an engineer.

"First, go with Angie and follow his lead to get to the Revenant without the yard supervisor seeing you. Get yourself set up in quarters aboard and both of you get a good night's sleep. I think we have a way around Ahriman's requisition.

"It's entirely possible the whole requisition thing is a bit of a dodge. The amount of money Ahriman would have to spend to lock up three ships like mine would be a budget buster. I think the requisition was a fake. For one thing, there was no counter-signature on it, and for a requisition that large, there'd have to be. And for another thing, if I'd just hopped a ship and left, if the requisition was real, he'd own a boat load of parts he'd have absolutely no use for and probably wouldn't be able to sell.

"No. The more I've thought about it, Sam Cogley, my lawyer, was right. He thinks Ahriman did the same thing to the yard supervisor that he did to Captain Wilson. He directed them both to stop me personally, to thwart whatever plans I made. It's personal with him, and he'd keep it that way. So he gave the yard supervisor the fake requisition and specific instructions to use it to shut me down.

"Tomorrow morning, check out the work I've already done and make sure everything is up to specs. Then, late afternoon, or even early evening, Miller, you head over to the supervisor's office and request the parts you'll need. Here's a list I made earlier. I've a reasonable hunch that if you don't tell him who it is for and just act like you do this kind of thing every day...maybe even suggesting that your ship is at one of the other yards, but they don't have the parts you need, he'll sell them to you and think he's outsmarted me again by getting rid of the parts to someone else."

Miller smiled. "I like it. It's a no risk thing for us. Either we get the parts or we don't. And if we don't, we are no worse off than we are right now."

"Right. Now on your way, gentlemen. Take care to keep some distance between you so you aren't seen together."

"Aye, Captain," said Miller, and whipped out a pretty sharp salute. That he was ginning spoiled it a bit, but then so was I when I returned his salute.

Over the next few weeks my plan worked. I stayed at the boarding house and well away from the ship, except at night when I could get there unseen. Angie's help and Miller's expertise cut our repair times by at least a third because he knew shortcuts and tricks that I didn't. We got all the parts we needed, no questions asked.

I think both Angie and Miller found the idea that we were a team rather than a captain and crew took a bit of getting used to. When I showed up after dark, I wasn't giving commands...I was presenting myself to get directions from them about what I needed to do. That was outside their experience, but they quickly saw the wisdom of deference to expertise and got over any hesitancy. I myself greatly preferred working together rather than working separately.

Most of the inboard systems got repaired fairly quickly and thoroughly tested early on. We could move apace on those because they were not visible to the outside world, and the tests were invisible to even specifically prying eyes. And knowing Ahriman, I was sure those were there.

Miller would buy parts in the early evening and make arrangements for them to be left on a loading dock for pick up later on. He had the yard supervisor believing he was "job siting" all the parts he would need for the next day's work at another yard. But after the supervisor left for the day, Angie and Miller would circle back, pick up the parts, and split up to approach the Revenant at different times from different directions to minimize detection.

During daylight hours, they'd be working inside the ship

installing and testing those parts.

Where it got dicey was when all the inside work was done and it left only outside work. That meant that there would be no more daytime work other than procuring parts. We would have to work outside, after dark, and all testing would have to be done carefully and potentially with some sort of diversion. It definitely taxed our creativity to come up with diversions that deflected attention off of us, but did not create suspicion that they were in fact artificial.

Eventually, it all was done, tested, and even improved upon. I don't think I've ever seen Miller that proud.

"She really is a Revenant, Cap," he said after the last engine test. "She was all but dead, but now she's alive."

I clapped them both on the shoulders. "Congratulation, boys. You've brought life to her. If I know ships at all, and I think I do, that means she'll be grateful to you from her bones to her skin. She'll take good care of you because you've taken good care of her."

It was dawn when I arrived at the boarding house. As I walked up the way, a large figure stepped out of the shadows into my path. "Sorry," I murmured and made to go around him.

"Not so fast, Sandborn. I've got a message for you."

"How do you know my name?"

"Never you mind what I know. Just listen and listen good. Ahriman has his eye on you. He knows you've got a contract to move some cargo. He doesn't like independents, and he especially doesn't like you. If you know what's good for you, you'll back out of this contract today."

"And if I don't?" I asked.

"If you don't, a couple of my friends and I will have an entirely different message for you this time tomorrow. And you definitely don't want to be on the receiving end of that message. Got it?"

"Yup. Got it." This guy was two of me, and I'm no small guy. I was expecting a little "love tap" to help drive the message home. I was not disappointed. I think I actually saw stars.

When the earth and sky righted themselves in my vision, and my brain began to function again, I looked around but the "messenger" was gone. I touched the left side of my face and it was tender from my jaw to my ear to my eye socket. That guy didn't have fists; he had mallets for hands.

I picked myself up off the sidewalk and made my way back to my room. I splashed water on my face, changed my clothes, and hurried out to meet with my cargo contractor. We were going to be leaving today...well before any pending "messages" coming my way.

Within three hours we were loading cargo on the Revenant. Thirty minutes after we loaded the last container, we had generated enough auxiliary power to fire the maneuvering thrusters to begin our ascent. All three of us were seated in the somewhat cramped bridge. Angie was at Navigation, Bucky was at Engineering, and I was in the pilot's seat. It took all three of us to fly her.

Within six minutes of initial lift off, we had reached a sufficient altitude to fire our sub-luminal engines to achieve escape velocity. Within eighteen minutes we were in planetary orbit, recharging our sub-luminal engines and maneuvering thrusters to make the leap into a flight path that would take us to our destination.

Forty-five minutes after that, we were at the apogee of our orbit, oriented according to Angie's calculations, and at full thruster and engine capacity.

"On my mark, fire all engines in a controlled burn for six minutes."

"Aye, Captain. Commencing six-minute burn on your mark." Bucky would initiate the burn from Engineering. It would take all my attention to keep the maneuvering thrusters oriented at the optimum angle to maintain the proper trajectory.

We couldn't use the jump drive this close to civilization. We were going to "leap" from orbit in a powerful push to give us enough initial space velocity to carry us as quickly as possible to a point where a jump could be attempted.

"Countdown commencing. Five. Four. Three. Ready. Steady. MARK!"

Instantly we were crushed back into our seats as the power from engines and thrusters kicked in at full force. As our initial inertia was overcome, the pressure on our bodies decreased some and we could move a bit in our seats. The roar of the burn was deafening.

"Burn at one minute in three, two, one. One minute." Bucky would count us through the six-minute burn cycle. Angie kept his eyes on the nav display and called out adjustments to me periodically. I just kept my eye on the instruments showing ship orientation and tried to keep it as steady as possible, not over-steering at Angie's course corrections.

"Burn at two minutes in three, two, one. Two minutes."

CRACK!

Angie's seat started to separate from its pedestal. He'd be thrown against the bulkhead.

"Angie! Your seat!" I called out, but then instantly wondered what he could possibly do while we were still pulling significant G forces.

"It'll hold, Deke. Come to port, zero point three five degrees."

"Port, zero three five, Pilot aye!"

"Burn at three minutes in three, two, one. Three minutes."

"Engineering! Nozzle temps!"

"Exhaust temps nominal, Captain. She'll hold together."

"I'm not totally convinced, Bucky. Keep an eye on it."

"Aye, Cap."

"Deke, you over compensated my last correction. Come starboard zero point zero zero five."

"Starboard, oh, oh, oh, five, Pilot aye! Sorry, Angie. Got distracted by the exhaust temps."

"Burn at four minutes in three, two, one. Four minutes."

CRACK! Another bolt on Angie's seat gave way.

"Angie!?!"

Loud and with authority: "Don't worry, Deke. It'll hold."

Much quieter and to himself: "C'mon, baby. Hold."

"Engineering! Fuel consumption?"

"Fuel consumption nominal, Captain. Fuel capacity more than sufficient." I heard Bucky bang a dial. "Uh, belay my last. Fuel capacity sufficient."

"Bucky!?!"

"Faulty dial, Cap. Stop worrying. We're good. We're all good."

"Burn at five minutes in three, two, one. Five minutes."

CRACK!

"I'm fine, Deke. Don't even ask. Still a bolt or two left."

"Engineering. Status."

"All systems, temps, and capacities nominal, Cap."

"Navigation. Report."

"Orientation, course, and speed all within tolerances, Deke."

Bucky called out, "Coming up on six, Deke!"

"Engineering. On your mark, cut all engines."

"Aye, Cap." A pause while Miller watched the clock. "Burn at six minutes and engine cut off at my mark. Five, four, three, ready, steady, MARK!"

Now the silence was deafening. Our ears screamed at the hissing that rang in them.

"Navigation. Report."

"Course 35.6 actual. Speed 39,600 kph relative. Spot on, Cap. Nice job on the stick, sir!"

"Good course and speed, Navigation. Great burn, Engineering. I declare the Cargo Ship Revenant operational and beautiful. Well done, crew. And by crew I mean me, too!"

It would take about 12 hours at this speed to get to where we could safely operate the jump drive. That system was totally rebuilt and totally untested. We all knew the outcome of that operation would determine one of three things.

If it operated properly, it would mean a successful jump and therefore a successful first half of our contract.

If it failed to operate, it would mean no jump at all, an unsuccessful first half of our contract, a long 12+ hour trip back to port, significant repairs, and most likely a run in with Ahriman's men.

Then there was always the third possibility. It would operate, but badly. That would mean our instant deaths inside the black hole we created.

CHAPTER 14 - **Transformation**

We didn't die.

Not on that trip, nor on the dozen that followed. That isn't to say everything was rainbows and butterflies. Like any older ship, the Revenant had her difficulties. With Miller's expertise, though, we could not just fix them, but actually improve each piece of equipment repaired.

Then there were the run-ins with Ahriman.

In nearly every port, small or large, we were challenged, threatened, and twice beaten up. The latter was aimed primarily at me, although Angie and Bucky were pushed around occasionally. Once we were even arrested and our cargo confiscated by local port authorities. Sam Cogley rode to our rescue and got the charges dismissed by the local magistrate and our cargo restored to us.

Coasties boarded us on so many occasions we lost count. Ahriman had significant influence there and used it. Nothing ever amounted to anything because unlike most independents, we actually had our act together. Our paperwork was always in order. Our safety protocols were documented. Our logs were up to date. Generally, we were as tight or tighter than even the Coasties themselves.

The one thing we had going for us that Ahriman could not wreck or tarnish was our reputation for on-time deliveries. Unlike our competitors, and there weren't many in our sector, if we told you we could get your goods where you wanted them on such-and-such a date, they arrived on time, with no losses. As that reputation grew, we could charge a bit more than the competition and get away with it.

Independents had a terrible reputation for having part of their shipments go "missing." It was more or less assumed that independents would pilfer a portion of the cargo to sell on their own to supplement their cargo fees. Shippers usually built in excess inventory to allow for that. We didn't do that. It wasn't because we were too good for that. It was that we knew if we did it, we'd get arrested and prosecuted and likely lose the Revenant. While the rest of the world turned a blind eye towards and even accommodated it, for us, they'd have made it a criminal act. Ahriman's intent was that focused.

Sure, it cost us more to run things that tight to the rules, but as harassed as we were, the cost to cut corners would have been much higher.

At the end of that twelfth run, we had paid off the lien on the ship and she was ours, free and clear. We were no longer tethered or accountable to our home port. We were free to go anywhere and take whatever contracts we wanted.

The three of us had crewed a ship that should have had five, better seven. We'd worked seven-day weeks and twelve-hour days seemingly without end. We were dead tired, but we were profoundly invested in what we'd done. We were happy. And such a word was never used to describe the crew of a cargo ship.

We would have preferred to add crew to our number, but

as long as we were based in Ahriman's home port, no one dared to join us. We'd asked. We'd recruited like mad. Secretly men would tell us they wanted to crew with us, but publicly they denied it. We were pariahs to them.

It was when we shifted our home port to Euridian, a smaller port but outside Ahriman's sector, that things loosened up. We had done a couple of runs to Euridian and so were a known entity there. The local port authority appeared benignly disinterested in us, but the local population of cargo sailors were very interested. At first glance, we appeared to be a prosperous ship and crew.

We were happy to take on two new crew members within the first week. Being our first experience with new crew, we didn't really know what to expect. Our shipboard regimen was so different from any other cargo ship, it was like the recruits were being immersed into an alien culture. The concept of mutual support and putting others before self was that foreign.

During the first few months, turnover in the crew was high. Some were just interested in enriching themselves. That wasn't a concept that was repugnant to us. After all, crew members had a right to expect to be paid both salaries and bonuses.

What was difficult for us, and ultimately for them, was how they did the work. Those that were only in it for themselves, usually former marine service types, found our approach difficult to swallow and insisted on being hyper competitive and demeaning of others. To them, the idea of mutual support was for suckers. Helping others got you nothing in return and even penalized you within a system set up to benefit the hyper-competitive. After a career of being rewarded by putting self over others, and even sabotaging the efforts of others, it was hard for them to see it any other way.

We welcomed them the same as any other crew member and gave them a chance to fit in. But our lack of self focus actually enhanced rather than lowered their suspicion we were gaming them. It got to the point we could tell pretty much from day one who was going to drop out early on.

Others started with a similar set of expectations, but rather quickly responded to the sense of camaraderie and mutual aid and benefit. It was a better way if you had eyes to see it. Some did.

When we reached our maximum crew of seven, turnover slowed down. The men who could embrace the culture wanted to stay. Crew openings became rarer, and we even had an informal waiting list of candidates.

Our business was growing faster with our increased capacity given a stable, full complement of crew. We found creative ways to increase cargo space and carry larger loads which allowed us to have a larger radius of what sectors we could serve. That in turn opened us up to cargo shippers of size, a group we might never have been able to work with as a short haul "local" company.

One of those shippers expressed a desire to partner with us to buy a larger ship...a ship larger even than the Rapacious. He would provide the capital and buy the ship if we would provide the shipping expertise. In exchange, we would give his cargo priority and a lower shipping charge. We talked about it and turned the offer down.

That was unheard of. The goal of all cargo business was to get ahead, make money, and ultimately buy a life of self-oriented leisure. We were saying no to a fast track to that end.

This was not someone who was used to hearing "no". He demanded to know our reasoning. It was simple, we explained. He would own the ship and ultimately we would have to operate the ship to his standard, his goal: self-enrichment. We understood that and had no trouble working with shippers who had that goal. But working *with* someone differs greatly from working *for* someone. Ultimately, you have to be what the person you work for wants you to be. We could not work for someone who had that goal.

Oh, we were interested in turning a profit, of earning more, even of self-enrichment. But none of that was the goal. Without even consciously thinking about it, our goal had become to create value for our clients...to provide excellent cargo services. Just as our goal as a crew had been to work together to make everyone's work better, without planning it, that became our approach to shippers we worked with. We found ourselves negotiating contracts by keeping the best interests of the shipper in mind. We were making money because every one of our shippers felt they were getting more in terms of service and response than they were paying in shipping fees.

We were, to put it succinctly, a "good deal". The moment we became more concerned with profit than service, all that would change. We would find ourselves taking advantage of shippers to maximize profits. As a result, our reputation would suffer and ultimately disappear, forcing us to have to compete with our peers on their terms after losing our competitive edge. We thanked the investor for the opportunity but refused the offer.

Then I made him a counter-offer. Buy the ship and give it to us.

The man's name was Butterman, Eldridge Butterman.

"Why that's preposterous! Idiotic! I'd be a total fool to do that! Out of the question! Why would I ever do such a thing?"

Miller spoke up, casting a quizzical eye at me as he spoke to Butterman. "I think what the Captain is suggesting, sir, is that if you do that, he'll do what you want and give you priority and discounted costs like you asked. And we'll do it for the life of the ship."

Butterman wasn't stupid. "And what assurance do I have that you'll do it…that you'll honor this agreement?"

Miller was smiling again. "Because we'll sign a binding contract to that effect. You get your lawyer to work it up and we'll get ours to check it out. If we sign it, we've got a deal. We'll even put the new ship up as collateral. If we renege on the terms, you get the ship back."

"And why would I do that?" Butterman was still not convinced.

Angie looked up. "Oh, you don't have to. This is just a suggestion. We've already told you we don't want your deal. So if you don't want ours, that's fine. We've got plenty of clients to keep us busy. And you'd still be one of them, uh, only without a discount or priority."

That was how we came to own the Revenant II.

Given its size, we suddenly went from needing a crew of seven to a crew of twenty-seven, or even more. The Revenant II was the big time. Cargos could be larger. Runs would become longer. Demands would be greater.

For a while we put the Revenant in "dry dock" while we focused on "the II" as she came to be known. We doubled the crew immediately and that was enough to scrape by for a while. We had the same turnover problems as before, but our reputation was better known, so some of the hard core folks didn't bother to apply.

Within a month, we were up to thirty crew members. Most of the guys got it. Some didn't but weren't turned off at the prospect of collaboratively working, even if they didn't understand it.

Within six months, we had enough crew to run both the Revenant and the II. It was at that point that I realized Angie, Miller, and I had something much more important going on than just a "new wave" cargo service.

We had become the beginning of a social movement.

People were coming to us and applying for work with no experience working in space in general or cargo in particular. A growing element of our crew were not professional or experienced. At first we hesitated in hiring what would otherwise have been considered "rookies." But when we hired our first couple just to get some "bodies" on board and saw the zeal with which they took to the work, and the transformation they experienced as they shed their preconceived perspectives of self; they blew away us.

There is nothing whatsoever romantic or enthralling about space cargo work. The romantics had long since realized that space cargo was the equivalent of 20th century Earthbound long haul trucking. It was long, tedious, not particularly rewarding, generally mind numbing, and definitely not exciting at all. But these people were flocking to us like we had found the magic to make it like some sort of swash-buckling adventure.

What was even more amazing was that their enthusiasm did not diminish when the reality of cargo handling and shipping set in. It didn't seem to faze them. They worked as hard or harder as our professional crew, shoulder to shoulder with them, but their attitudes never faltered.

It was the work that drew them, not some idea of adventure. We could have been a trash to energy plant and it wouldn't have mattered to them. There was freedom in what they were doing. They had to work, but the need for income was not what brought them to us. They were working with us because they wanted to work our way. The work itself had become its own reward.

It generally takes me a while to figure stuff out...an eternity of eternities in the chair, it seems. This was no exception. Eventually it dawned on me that it wasn't the work itself. It was how the work was done. They weren't doing anything different from any other cargo ship, but they were doing it differently. That was what was driving them. And apparently the word was getting out. The difference was becoming a topic of conversation. It wasn't a secret Angie, Bucky, and I held anymore. It was public knowledge.

Soon others came to us, not primarily for the work at all, but willing to do it to experience what was happening, to be changed. They specifically came to Euridian looking for us, seeking us out. They signed on, not caring in the least what we asked them to do, only caring that we let them do it with us. They weren't looking for a career or a long-term gig. They wanted to sign on for a run or two, as mess rats or engine wipers or ordinary deck hands...the lowest positions on the ship. And they felt like we had given them a gift in letting them do the most menial of jobs.

When their "contracts" were completed and they left the ship, they left as changed people. They left with a new view of the world around them. They went back to what they were doing before. They didn't do anything different. They did it differently.

Some faltered and faded. Some started back at their old positions with new zeal and understanding, but eventually succumbed to the pressure to conform to the status quo. But others did not. They created little oases of mutuality in their worlds. They drew others to themselves and taught the value of helping and serving by example.

It was as Angie had said. It was a virus...a good virus. And it was spreading.

All of this happened to us and around us, but we still were just thinking of ourselves as a cargo service. Maybe there were aspects of what we did which were the seeds of social change, but that was accidental...an unintended by-product of doing what we were doing. Yes, we were the beginning, but we were not the center of it. We were just shipping cargo.

And then there was the day that Brice Wilson arrived in Euridian. That was the day the truth became unavoidable.

CHAPTER 15 - **Back to Eden**

Our business had grown in such size and complexity that I could no longer travel on cargo runs. With both the Revenant and the II in continuous operation, someone had to set up an office and a point of contact for the administration of existing business and a place for new clients to get in contact with us. That someone was me. Bucky took over the captain position on the II and Angie headed up the Revenant. They both had good crews by this point, and both were running more or less at capacity.

I looked up from the seemingly never-ending paperwork to see Brice standing there in the doorway, in civvies, with a look of such intensity on his face it scared me.

I was frozen. Apparently he was, too. We looked at each other, eye to eye, for several long moments, waiting for one, the other, or just something to break the silence. Finally, he moved his fist to his mouth and coughed.

"Deke."

"Brice."

"I need to talk to…." "What brings you…". We both started

sentences at the same time. It broke down the tension and we both chuckled. "Go ahead," I said.

"Deke, I need to talk to you about something. I don't know how to do it. But I know I need to."

"What about, Brice?" I had more than a good idea where this conversation was going to go, but I knew it was important for Brice to say what he had to say in his way.

"Well, if you'd asked me that about a month ago, I'd have said it was about you and your boneheaded, scatterbrained, stupid business you're running. You're breaking all the unwritten rules...rules that we were taught by example and led to believe were the only way to success. And you've sucked others like Ariti and Miller into it, making my life hard and leaving me short-handed.

"If you'd ask me a couple of days ago, I'd have said it was about how dangerous what you're doing is...that it is putting at risk the fundamental basis of trade and enterprise in this sector...that you're foolhardy, stubborn, and engaged in a kind of tyranny that is going to put us out of business and destroy the wealth of many...including my chance at it.

"But now that I'm standing here, looking at you, face to face, all I can think to say is that I'm sorry and to ask you to forgive me. How's that for having a good handle on things?"

He wasn't done, and I wasn't going to cut to the chase just yet. He needed to get to the heart of it. "Forgive you for what, Brice?"

"Oh, that's just not fair! You're playing dumb just to get me to say it out loud. Is it that important, Deke, that I vocalize my humiliation?"

"No, Brice, it isn't. You have my forgiveness already and instantly...and in fact you've had it all along for everything. But that isn't because I am so good and you're so bad. You're not bad, and neither am I. We were both captives in a system that used us against each other. The system set us against one another to control us and keep us under its thumb.

"And, Brice, it isn't because I've had to spend weeks if not months figuring out how to forgive myself for the things I'd done to others, and maybe more importantly, the things I'd not done for others that I could or should have. And that includes you.

"No, it's because I was wrong about so many things I believed and lived for. You are, too. We thought life was about competing and winning. We thought life was about amassing the most and the quickest. And we were wrong. I learned life is about finding meaning in everything I do, and that meaning has to be something more than my own wealth and wellbeing. Those are not goals. At best, they're by-products of what we choose to do with the life we've been given.

"Brice, I have made so many bad choices in my life because I only chose for my own benefit. I learned that even if I won, I lost. I tallied the value of my life in my bank balance and the value of what I possessed. And in the end, it was all worthless. Worse, it was pointless.

"So, Brice, I'll ask again. Forgive you for what?"

"Deke, how do I put it in words? Those last few months, after Debris, when you were working with all the crew members, I watched you. At first I was angry because I thought you were engineering a coup by currying the favor of the crew. But you never used that favor to further any design that I could see.

"The ship honestly never ran better. And that made me mad that you could get that kind of effort out of the crew as a suspended and disgraced officer, and I couldn't as captain.

"Then I was furious when you left and it all fell apart because I had no clue what you did and couldn't begin to replicate it myself.

"I think maybe mostly I was angry and disappointed in

myself that I threw you off the ship in order to insure my own position as captain. You, who had done nothing in those months to deserve anything other than respect...and even loyalty, got nothing but disrespect and dishonor from me. Days later I realized I owed my captainship to an act of dishonor rather to any skill or capability on my part. I was ashamed. And I've never, ever felt shame in my life. It shouldn't have mattered how I became captain, but it did. You were more of a captain working shoulder to shoulder with the crew than I ever was or would be issuing orders from on high.

"Deke, it rocks my entire world that I even think in terms of forgiveness, but I know I need it. Forgiveness for what, you ask? For everything, Deke. For my whole life up to this moment. For everything."

"I forgive you, Brice."

We both stood there and looked at each other. I think Brice was expecting some thunder clap of change, some pulling back of the clouds and a bright light shining. But there was nothing. He just stood there, looking at me looking at him.

"Huh. I thought there'd be something, Deke."

I reached out and gently put my hand on his shoulder. "There will be. There will be. All you've done is erase the slate. It's clean...wiped clean. But nothing new has been written on it yet. That's why this seems sort of strange right now. You're thinking this is the culmination of some great realization...a pinnacle of understanding. In one sense, it is. But in another, much more profound sense, it is the lowest point of your life. It is you at zero. What you do next is what matters, not anything you did before."

"I'm leaving the service, Deke. I decided when I left the Rapacious this morning that I was done. When I go back, I'm resigning my commission. Have you got room for one more crew member?"

"No, Brice. I don't." He looked up at me suddenly, shocked.

"What? I'm standing here quite literally with my hat in my hands asking for help from the person who I have seen help everyone, and you're saying 'no'?"

"I didn't say I wouldn't help you. I said you can't be part of my crew. Instead, I want you to be a passenger. But first I need you to go back to the Rapacious and forward a request to Ahriman for 60 days of leave. I know you've probably got it. Don't resign. Take a trip with us and if you still want to resign when we get back, you can do it. OK?"

"I don't want a vacation! I want answers, Deke."

"Oh, where I'm taking you is anything but a vacation. It'll be the hardest work you ever did, ever, in your whole life. Will you do it?"

Brice looked like a man who'd proposed marriage and instead of getting a yes, got an offer of free steak knives.

"Do I have a choice?" Brice asked.

"Sure," I said. "You can do what I asked or you can resign and go join some other pirate outfit or you can go back to being captain of the Rapacious. You just can't have the one thing you think you really want. But I think you'll find that when we get back, you will be glad I didn't say yes."

There was nothing left to say. Brice had humbled himself to come and ask for forgiveness from me. Doing what I asked was just a single step further in that path of humility. It wasn't humiliation; it was humbleness. I don't think at this point he really knew what the difference was. Then again, I don't think he really cared. He left to go back to the Rapacious to do as I'd asked.

Brice was a man at the end of himself. He had nowhere else to go. If I had agreed to take him on as crew, I would have been taking advantage of him, using him for my own benefit. But if he was willing to do what I asked him to do, it would set him on a very different path...one suited to him.

Don't think I was so smart that I already knew what that path was. I didn't. I just somehow knew his path wasn't mine, and I knew where Brice could go to find out what it was.

I quickly fired off two messages.

Begin Message
To: A. Ariti, Captain Revenant
RE: Change in plans
Message: Angie, put the Revenant in dry dock and bring your crew aboard the II. Miller will have new orders.

Please acknowledge

End Message

***

Begin Message
To: B. Miller, Captain Revenant II
RE: Change in plans
Message: Miller, make room for Ariti and his crew. Then come by my office and pick up some old star charts I have here. You're going to need them. We're going to Debris.
End Message

It just so happened that both ships were in port at the same time...something of a rarity. Since we were going to be gone for the better part of 60 days, I figured it would be best to have the Revenant in dry dock rather than just leaving it moored in space. That took the better part of a day to get that done. By the afternoon of the second day, we were ready for departure.

Technically Brice and I were both passengers as we were not on the crew of either ship. It was a pointless distinction since everyone knew I was going to pitch in wherever I could. Brice, whether through following my example or just to escape the boredom of the trip, did likewise. The combined crew were already well acclimated to our collegial work style, so they not only accepted Brice but helped him fit in.

Brice had always been a technically proficient officer, and as a captain had adjusted to command with a measure of grace. He was definitely no Ahriman. He didn't bully or belittle. But he was also not me. He carried an air of authority and privilege which caused him to be a bit standoffish. As the trip progressed, however, I watched that slough off slowly. By the time we reached Debris, it was mostly gone. He still had an air of rank, but he wore it like a soiled work shirt.

It didn't take as long to get to Debris on the II as it had to get back from Debris on the Rapacious. Partly that was because we were confident in the ability of our jump drives and could take larger "bites" of the space-time field. But it was also due to the fact we had slightly newer jump drives and a multi-talented crew that kept them in the most efficient state I'd ever seen. One of the great consequences of teamwork is shared knowledge and expertise. Our crews had become cross trained in pretty much all major systems voluntarily. Each crew member had a designated job and set of responsibilities for a shift. However, most utilized at least some of their time off the shift by partnering with and helping other crew members, and so learned different skills. In fact, some of the crew started calling that time "Revenant University."

It also meant that dissension and friction between individual crew members was minimal if it existed at all. Crew morale was the best it could be. When the crew saw the value of shared tasks, getting angry at someone carried a price tag of separation and loss of help. Anger and arguing quickly had morphed from being a regular element of crew life, to being a luxury the crew could not afford, finally to being a totally useless futility.

In the present situation, this meant Brice was not left sitting in his quarters with nothing to do and no one to talk with. The crew accepted him as one of their own even though he had no assigned duties. He worked with all of them at one time or another during the passage. He ate with them. And the liveliness of shared friendship based on a common objective washed over him like a balm.

We talked a bit during the passage, but not much since his time was taken up by the crew. I didn't avoid conversations with him at all. It just seemed to me for him to be exposed to this for himself rather than having me tell him about it was a far better experience.

What we never talked about even when we did talk was why we were going to Debris. Brice knew that Debris was the source of my transformation, but he didn't know why. He'd asked one of the first times we'd found a chance to chat on this trip, but I put him off. It was too long a story and it would create too many questions I wasn't prepared to answer.

The only person I had ever told about the chair was Angie. I hadn't even told Miller. The evidence of the chair had been my changed life, but by now, that change had replicated itself in dozens if not a hundred or more others. None of them knew about the chair. They just knew about this new way.

But now, here was Brice, and I knew he had to experience the chair for himself. Why? I didn't have the answer to that question. I just knew it was not for me to explain it to him. It was for him to experience it himself, first hand, with no preconceived notions.

We landed on Debris, descending through that familiar deep dark grayness, and found the original landing spot of the Rapacious. I left orders with the crew to hang around the II for the rest of the "day" while Angie, Miller, and Brice went with me to the city.

If felt strange to do this again, like a dream. I led them through the outlying houses, the outskirts of the city, and eventually through the park filled with statues, to the strange translucent building. The chair was still there. Unmoving. Seemingly inert. Harmless.

"Brice, I told you once that when the time was right I would talk to you about my change. You were curious. You wanted to know what changed me. I put you off then, but no longer. It was this chair, Brice. It changed me. And if you want to understand how and why, sit in it."

"No!" said Brice and whirled around and walked out of the building.

CHAPTER 16 - **The Chair Again**

I followed Brice out into the darkness. He was breathing heavily, not from any exertion, but I could see his breath as a dark, vaporous shadow. He had stopped a few paces from the building. His back was to me and his head was down.

"Brice?"

No answer.

"Brice, what's up?"

Still no answer.

"Are you scared?"

"Hell yes, I'm scared. A chair? Really? What is it, an electric chair?"

"No, Brice, it's not. I sat in it and I'm still here."

"Oh, that's very comforting. You sat in it and it turned your whole view of the world upside down. Yeah, that's very comforting. For all I know, it scrambled your brains, and it was just by the luck of the draw you ended up sane but upside down. If I sit in it, I could end up an idiot or a moron or, worse, a fool. Not doing it! Not doing it!"

"That's not going to happen, Brice."

"Oh?   Can you guarantee me that?   Can you put that in writing? No. And even if you could, it would be a worthless guarantee because if it happened, and I became a fool there is nothing you could do to reverse that. I would be a blithering fool."

"OK. I understand. If you do not want to experience the chair, you don't have to. I brought you here because I believe, firmly, that the answers you seek are here, in that chair. When I sat in it, it answered questions for me I didn't even know I had.   But that doesn't matter.   That was my experience, and any assurances I could give you would be based on a single trial...my trial of the chair. No matter how much I can accept that as the truth of the chair, you may not. I get it. It's too great a risk, too big a leap. I'll go back to the II with you."

I turned to head back the way we came and took a couple of tentative steps. Brice never moved. I stopped. I waited in the semi-darkness.

"Deke?"

"Yeah, Brice."

"I can't go back. I know I'm supposed to be here."

I didn't answer.

"I know I'm supposed to be here," he repeated.

I still did not answer.

"I KNOW I'm supposed to be HERE, Deke."

"What do you want to do, Brice?"

"What do I want to do?" he accented the "I". "Me? I want to bolt. I want to go back to the ship and leave. I want to pretend like I was never here. I want to go back to the way things were, where I was captain because I had won, I had beaten everyone else out of the job, I was on top. That's what 'I' want."

"And?" I asked.

"And it doesn't matter what I want. Not now. Not here.

Not in this place. This is the place of darkness, Deke. This is the place where what I want doesn't matter. I hate this place. But I cannot leave any more than I could flap my arms and fly.

"I'm caught between two outcomes. I can sit in the chair and risk death or worse, risk becoming a fool; or I can walk away and go back to my old life like a dead man because I know I'm not supposed to do that. Either way, in a sense, I die."

"It's your choice, Brice. It always has been. You get to choose. You can go further in or further out. Death via the chair or death via a thousand regrets. It's your choice."

I heard the gravel under Brice's boots as he turned and walked back into the building.

In the end, all three sat in the chair. First Brice, then Ariti, and lastly Miller.

Miller was the only one to talk after waking up.

"It was wonderful, Deke!" I had never seen such a serenity in anyone. His face literally shone with peace and joy.

"I lived my whole life, my whole, long life just now. I worked for you, Deke, for a long time. Then I left and went off on my own. Along the way, I got married and had children and my wife and I raised them to be fine young men and women. I loved my wife fiercely. I lived my life and faced everything that came at me. I wasn't perfect. I made some bad choices, but many, many more good choices. In the end, I had helped many, many friends and co-workers. It felt good, Deke. Even with the mistakes, when I got to the end and my kids had moved away and my wife had gone before me, I knew at that last breath at the last moment at that last day, I had done it right. And then I died. And I spent an eternity in…in…I can't describe it, Deke. What? A warm embrace? Yeah, maybe that's what it was, a warm, gentle, wonderful embrace. I'm almost sorry I had to come back from it to tell you about it."

"Bucky, that's amazing," I said.

"Yeah, amazing. To have lived my life and experienced it all and been given the chance to get it right. It was amazing. It is amazing even now. I wish I had the words to say it all so you'd know. Thank you, Deke, for bringing me to this place. For showing me the chair through your life. I am so grateful.

"But Deke, don't feel bad about what's going to happen. I'm supposed to tell you it's not your fault. I need to tell you, it's not your fault. Don't feel bad, Deke. I promise, it's not your fault."

"What's not my fault, Bucky?"

He didn't answer. He just smiled, still sitting in the chair. He looked at each of us and smiled.

And then he died.

No one had spoken before. No one spoke now. Whatever work the chair had done with Wilson and Ariti, if any, remained with them. I scooped Miller up in my arms. He seemed light to me, almost no burden at all. And almost as if on cue, we all walked back to the II.

Everyone knew about Miller's disease. It wasn't that it was a topic of conversation. It was that his crews needed to know about it so they were prepared for that event whenever it happened. As we approached the II, most of the crew was outside. They saw the form in my arms and they knew Bucky was gone.

Those that had hats, doffed them. Those that didn't, bowed their heads as though in prayer. A few reached out to touch him as we passed. No one spoke. Everyone knew.

I laid Bucky in his Chief's bunk for one last night. I told the crew we would meet outside in what passed for morning for a few words for Captain Miller and his interment.

The next morning, with everyone assembled and

respectfully silent, I told them everything. I told them of the chair, my time in the chair and its impact on me. I told them that Brice and Ariti had sat in the chair as well, but were not ready to talk about it yet. And I told them about Bucky and his time in the chair and the wonderful things he had said.

I told them that the chair didn't kill Bucky, his disease did. The chair hadn't killed him at all. In fact, it had given him the greatest gift that Bucky could have possibly been given: the chance to live his entire life, complete with career and love and family and ups and downs and everything. And it gave it to him because what he brought to the chair was the knowledge that he was probably never going to be able to live long enough to do any of that. Bucky got to live his whole life.

I told them that the chair wasn't magic or a mystery. I told them that the chair took whatever a person brought to it, revealed it and reflected it back to the person, and made them experience the consequences of the choices they were making.

I told them the chair was created by a race of beings that discovered the value of a second chance. I tried to explain that when someone truly understands the cost of the choices they make, good or bad, and then gets the chance to experience the ramifications of those choices in eternity, and THEN gets the chance to wake up from that eternity and start all over again, that it wasn't really a second chance. It was really dying and being reborn.

It was a genesis: a new beginning.

We buried Bucky on Debris, near to the outskirts of the town. And then I offered every person on that ship the opportunity to sit in the chair. They all did.

The trip back to Euridian was quiet. At first, the crew did not talk to one another; the experience of the chair was still too new, too raw. It takes time to assess the futility you've created in your own life. It takes more time to begin the process of turning it around. The crew had one advantage I had not had on my trip from Debris: they had already developed the practice of helping one another. They fell into it like a regimen, a healthy, good regimen. But now they realized that the choices they were making to help and support one another, to choose others over themselves, were not just good habits. There was an eternal weight to those choices. They weren't sacred or religious or anything like that. They were just heavy and meaningful, and not to be lightly taken.

Before, they had been emulating the examples they had seen around them. It felt good. Everyone was doing it. Doing it was easier than not doing it. There was understanding of the principle, but no ownership. Now they were realizing within themselves the power of the choice. The reality of the choices and what it meant for the future, their future, was real. This weight, this gravity was new to them.

Maybe for the first time in their lives they began to know the real meaning of duty. All their adult lives, at least for those in the service, they were told to do their duty. What that really meant was do your job, perform the duties assigned to you. But there is a higher concept of duty they were coming to grips with…duty as an obligation that existed independently of self-interest, and not infrequently in conflict with it. Real duty required them to accept the fact that there were obligations in their lives that were not of their own choosing, but that they had to accept nonetheless. Real duty required them to consider the cost to others of not doing their duty. Real duty required them to think of others first.

It is sobering to realize the extent of your miscalculations in life. And where we had been giddy on our trip to Debris, we were sober on our return. It took several days, but eventually I could hear snippets of conversations among the crew as they began to share their experiences in the chair. At first they were tentative and revealed only pieces of what they'd gone through. But as the commonality of everyone's experience became more evident, the sharing became more robust.

They got beyond the fear that their experience would be so different from others that we would think them weird. They saw that while the details were unique; the outcomes were the same. And in the sharing, I could see a bond being birthed between all of them. It wasn't a bond of shared experience, because each had had uniquely individualized experiences. No two were alike in content. It was that they were all changed in the same way. What was common was what they had become. The flow of their lives had been reversed. Instead of using their strength to bring benefit to themselves, they were drawing on themselves to bring benefit to others.

One of the crew, a young man named Stephen, gave perhaps the best explanation.

"Deke, it is like all my life up to now there has been a black hole in my gut sucking in everything that got near me. But now there is this white hole that is like a fountain spewing out things from me. I think I might be physically sick if I tried to put a lid on it."

What was ironic to me was that all these crew members had been doing this "giving" thing since they joined us, well before Debris. Now, after Debris, they were still doing the same things, but with greater seriousness. The test of whether you are doing something by example or commitment is what you do when no one is watching. Before Debris, I had always been unsure if the way we worked would stay with them when they left the Revenant. But now I knew, as I watched these people, they were changed. It was coming from some internal motivation. It would not stop should they leave.

We were most of the way back when Angie and Brice came to me wanting to talk. The resulting conversation was long, very long, measured in hours. I will not set it all down here, but I will tell you what they said as I understood it.

When Angie sat in the chair, it took him back to his first years in the merchant service and he literally watched himself live all those years all over again. Somehow he was like a passenger in his own body and brain. He was reliving everything, making the same decisions, taking the same actions in one part of his consciousness, but the other part was an observer, simply watching what was happening.

Angie's career had been helping people as a mess rat and then steward. But now, with this ability to step outside of himself, he saw what was really going on. He was a mouse in an experiment. The light would come on, he would press the lever, and he would get the piece of cheese. Only the light was seeing something that someone needed to have done, the lever was doing it, and the rewards were promotion. Promotion wasn't the same thing for Angie as it had been for me. For him, he had chosen to be mess rat. But as he did his job more and better, the people he was assigned to do it for became higher and higher ranking. Angie's standard of living as a crew member was intimately related to the standard of living of those he served. If you served the crew, you had no better than the crew. But if you served the captain…. Angie had progressed, but like that mouse, he had no real connection with the light or the lever. He couldn't have cared less about the need or the person. It was all about the reward…getting ahead.

The chair allowed him to see how close to being dead in his heart he really came. The chair showed him what death was like had he died before I came back to Rapacious from the chair and modeled another way. He spent an eternity like me…cold and alone.

He got the point like no one else. It was never about what you do. He'd served others all his adult life, but he didn't get any better eternity than I did who served no one before the chair. Angie got it. It's never about what you do; it's always about why you do it.

Brice was a totally different story.

Where I had died repeatedly, Brice only died once. But in the chair he experienced an almost immortal life span of only one life. He lived more than 900 years, aging but never really growing old. He outlived everyone many times over. He married, had children, raised them, and one by one they died yet he lived, and then he married again. He had perhaps a dozen families before he resisted marrying again. He began to change his name and move to hide his identity and disguise his agelessness. He lived so long he became tired of living and longed for death.

In his life, although not dying and being reborn/brought back over and over again as had happened to me, he nonetheless experienced the opportunity to try to get it right over and over again. Only without death, he never could see the true weight of his choices. He was moved only by some vague, internal sense that in each generation he survived, he wasn't getting it "right" but he didn't know why. He lived through 900 years of trial and error.

I shuddered as I listened to him as it struck me how futile life can be without an external "yardstick" to help us find our way. For me, I knew what the ramifications of my choices were, because I experienced them with each death. For Brice, he wandered through centuries of guessing and assuming but never really knowing.

And then death came, suddenly and unexpectedly, taking him amid some life circumstance. He was alone by choice having shunned relationships he was destined to outlive. He had become a veritable hermit. He was, and then in a moment, he was no more.

Where death for me had been an eternity of cold nothingness, eternity was filled him with memories of his entire life. It was indescribable, he said, but it felt like being in an infinite museum of his life with exhibit after exhibit of events he'd lived through, each one brightly lit. He spent eternity walking through this "museum" and contemplating each exhibit. And as it was eternal, he walked through it a seemingly infinite number of times, visiting and revisiting each exhibit.

As he did, he realized some exhibits gave him peace and some regrets.

He began to understand what the common denominator was in the exhibits that brought peace. In each, his action was based on his genuine love for and desire to help others. As he came to those exhibits, his heart would swell and the loneliness of eternal death lifted a bit.

As he came to the other exhibits, it moved him to apologize to those representations of others in his life that were frozen in the frozen time of those exhibits. As he apologized for his selfishness, the lights of those exhibits began to tone down. Eventually, and this took a very long time according to Brice, those exhibits became totally dark while the ones that gave him peace remained brightly lit.

From that point on, he walked only in the light of the exhibits that shone with kindnesses.

And that was when the chair brought him back.

CHAPTER 17 - **Family**

Once back on Euridian, we had to reorganize. Without Bucky, we did not have a second captain besides me, so Angie took over the II and I would captain the Revenant for jobs that couldn't be handled, for whatever reason, by the II. Sometimes a cargo was too small to handle profitably on the II. Sometimes we were hired to transport individuals, like a passenger service, although it was definitely not First Class. If anonymity was needed, a hired cargo transport like the Revenant fit the bill. Where we had been running the Revenant full time, we decided to put it in reserve until it was needed for a specific run so I could continue to operate the business from the office most of the time without the need to spend too much time in space.

Brice? Oh, he took my advice and went back to the Rapacious. It was a hard thing to do, but he knew that was where he was supposed to be. We stayed in contact…a lot. Somehow the chair made us like family. When we sidelined the Revenant, we ended up with half a dozen crew looking for jobs. He took them on.

From all reports, when those men went to the Rapacious, they made a striking impact on ship's morale. Most of the Rapacious' hardened crew had no idea what to do with them, but with the captain watching out for them, they became seeds of a better way of life. It took some time, but the Rapacious began to operate much like the Revenant.

In turn, when we needed crew, Brice would send some of his harder core crew over to us. We were always glad to have the help, even if they weren't always glad to be there. In most cases we had a positive impact on them.

That was when it dawned on me that perhaps the better use for the Revenant, when schedules allowed, was making the occasional trip to Debris with such a crew. It got to be almost like a bootcamp. New crew would show up and for six weeks they'd work shoulder to shoulder with the existing crew, learn the new ways of working together, and eventually grow to appreciate it. The older hands of our crew would take those new to us under their wings, and before long the stories of Debris and the chair would work their way into the conversation.

By the time they'd become a fully functioning crew member, they were curious enough about the chair to want to make the trip. I was always happy to oblige. I don't remember that anyone refused to sit in the chair on those trips.

Having landed on Debris twice so far, we had become convinced Debris' position in space was "fixed". It was a rogue planet because it was not part of any solar system, but it was not your typical rogue planet that found itself zipping through space on its own. It simply defied the laws of planetary mechanics and just stayed put where it was.

As the months turned into years, our "family" grew. And space crews being space crews, they didn't always stay with either Angie and the II or Brice and the Rapacious. They found other jobs, they grew up and out. Euridian was the epicenter of a growing, spreading family of people changed by the chair. I suppose we were a movement. We had all the earmarks of one.

The good news for us was that wherever we traveled, there seemed to be a small nucleus of individuals who made themselves known to us and helped us in whatever ways they could. Some were old crew members of ours. Some were the families of those crew members. Others were people who knew some of our "scattered crew" and were "second generation". They were following the examples that had been set for them or taught to them by the first generation, but had not been to the chair themselves.

The bad news was that the more of us there were, the more disruptive we were of the status quo. Understand that the economy and culture of the day was based on raw ambition. Heroes and leaders were not good people, they were "winners", and they owed their wealth, prestige, and power to the system they had used to climb to the top. They controlled those under them by intimidation and through rewarding selfish individualism. We were the polar opposite, and eventually in certain sectors, we began disrupting that system. When people were no longer driven by the need to succeed, the power of success dissipated.

What was motivating our people was more "tidal" than individual. There was still a desire to improve one's life and get ahead, just not at the expense of others. Instead, by helping others who in turn were helping back, everyone was progressing together.

The ruling elite were losing control over a small but significant and growing element of the population. To be a member of that elite, one needed to demonstrate a control over those beneath you. When that was threatened, whatever caused that threat had to be eliminated.

We were that threat.

At first it was just verbal intimidation, threats, and innuendo. But as our influence grew, the verbal confrontations became physical. Our crews were assaulted from time to time, robbed occasionally, or saw relatives and family members lose their jobs for no good reason.

We always gave our crew members the freedom to quit at any time they felt the price was too high to pay. Very few did. All of them had experienced at least one eternity in the chair, so to them the stakes were eternal, and at some point trading the eternal weight of what you were doing for temporary respite was just a bad deal.

Eventually, we found our customers canceling contracts at the last minute for no reason, at least no reason they were prepared to give us. We knew why. Local governmental and business leaders were threatening them if they didn't move their business elsewhere.

No one was immune from the harassment…least of all me. Ahriman had identified me as the center of this disruptive influence, and so I drew special ire. Ahriman's reach went beyond the service into local port authorities and businesses. As the person who controlled merchant crews, he essentially controlled commerce, and that gave him leverage on every aspect of remote colonies.

I was breaking no laws, but that did not stop the authorities from arresting me, holding me for days in a jail, and then prosecuting me for whatever they could find to use. Since I was breaking no law, it was never possible to force me to stop doing what I was doing. But I paid outrageous fines and spent days in jail and forfeited profits on numerous runs due to trumped up charges on the pettiest of crimes.

I once was fined the entire profit from a run for allegedly corrupting a minor. A warehouse owner had left his 15-year-old son in charge while he went to get some lunch. He apparently had a few too many "beverages" with lunch and ended up in the local lockup until he sobered up. In the meantime, the cargo was due to be split up between four recipients and they were using the warehouse to sort it out. They were all there. We unloaded the cargo, but the 15-year-old had to sign the bill of lading to make the transfer legal. The cargo was alcohol, the drinking kind. He never actually even touched the cargo, and none of it stayed in his warehouse for more than an hour.

When the legal recourses failed to do more than just inconvenience us, and the peer pressure on our clients failed to dry up our business sufficiently, the authorities turned a blind eye to the more physical abuses foisted on us. It got to the point where I could not set foot on certain planets. And on one too many occasions, the severity of the attacks almost ended my life. I was not even safe on Euridian anymore.

I tried to talk to Ahriman. I knew he was the key driver behind all this. He could not stand to allow me to compete with him on any level. I took my life in my hands and visited his office on three occasions. On two of them I was left waiting for hours until the office closed and I was forced to leave. On the third occasion he saw me, but he threatened to kill me if I did not stop, dissolve the business, and sell the assets. He was a man possessed. There was no reasoning with him, nor was there any reason in him.

All this time, we continued to make trips to Debris in the Revenant with seven or eight passengers at a time, sometimes as many as 20 crowded in. They all came back changed. They all lived their lives in ways far different than they had before.

It was then that Ahriman hit upon the idea that would stop me completely. I should have seen it coming.

His name was Sein. And in retrospect, even if I'd been looking for pretenders, I wouldn't have seen it in him.

Cargo crews are a motley bunch. They come in all ages, sizes, and genders. Most captains don't bother to do a background check on potential crew members. If they look like they can do the work and swear they are the right age, they're in. As a captain, I'd gotten to be a pretty good judge of character...and gender...and age over the years. But I was not prepared for this.

In one cohort of crew we were hiring, I went through the usual hiring process and determined they were all suitable candidates. They had papers that were in order, or at least they seemed so to me. I hired them en masse. Sein came up to me afterwards, pulled me aside from everyone else, and asked when the next trip to Debris was, and could he be on it.

We did not talk about Debris outside of our own numbers. Just like I learned on those first few days on the Rapacious when I came back from the chair, there was no value in sharing it. Angie had nailed it: you were going to be thought weird just by acting so different. There was no sense compounding it with a super weird story of some chair and multiple eternities.

So it was rare that anyone came to us asking specifically about Debris. But it wasn't unheard of, either. So while this kid raised a red flag or two, he wasn't so far out of the norm as to motivate me to undertake any further scrutiny.

Most of the time new crew members worked a few runs before they were told of the chair and were offered the chance to go to Debris. Like this kid, occasionally one would come to us specifically to go to Debris, and I was willing to oblige if he or she seemed sincere. Sein seemed sincere.

So we shoehorned him in on the next Debris run. Strangely, when we got there, he elected not to sit in the chair which caused me to scratch my head since he'd already known about Debris and had asked to go. Stranger still, when we got home to port, Sein disappeared almost immediately.

The next day, Coasties boarded the Revenant and arrested me on charges of abduction, kidnapping a minor.

Sam Cogley came to Euridian to represent me at the trial, but in the end, there was little he could do. Sein was a minor, and his testimony was that I had tricked him into forging his paperwork and signing on as crew. He said I had promised him a whole host of things that would turn a young boy's head. None of it was true, of course, but since no one but me had interviewed him, and none of the other recruits had heard anything he had said to me about wanting to go to Debris, it was essentially my word against his.

Sein was a young boy. I was a former, disgraced mariner and now "pirate". In the old, old days, what Sein said I did would have been close to "Shanghai", what pirates often did, taking a captive while they are unaware. No jury was going to find for me over him. I was found guilty and sentenced to 20 years in prison.

At Sam's advice, I appealed. Since we were in deep space, there was no appellate court available. The appeal would have to be heard on Earth. They remanded me into Coastie custody for transport back to Earth.

I had a day or two before travel arrangements could be made and I did my best to put affairs in order. Angie was my almost constant companion during those last few days.

"I understand, Deke. I can handle the II and we can put the Revenant in dry dock until you get back. We've got a core of good crew now, and I can see one or two that could be captain material before too long. We'll keep things moving while this works out."

Angie hadn't given up hope that the jury verdict would be overturned on appeal.

"Angie, I'm not putting you in charge. I'm telling you the II and the Revenant are yours. Sam is completing the paperwork today to put them both in your name. We have to face the reality that unless we find some new evidence, this appeal is going to fail. I may never be coming back. I'm giving it all to you."

"Don't even think that, Deke. It has to work out. You're innocent. Anyone with half a brain knows this was a setup."

"Angie, you know it, and I know it, but for everyone else it has to be proven. And in the case of a crime against a minor, the principle might be innocent until proven guilty, but the reality is guilty until proven innocent."

Angie was crestfallen. We had been a team since the Rapacious and in his adult life he had always had a superior officer to follow. Now he was going to be the superior officer, and frankly, that scared him.

"Deke, I don't know that I can do this."

"Angie, you were made for this. Your entire DNA is geared toward helping others. It is not just what you do, it is who you are. What if, Angie, leaders were not men and women who led by precept and by issuing orders? What if leadership wasn't 'being in charge' but rather enabling your crew to do their jobs as best they can? What if the best leaders were the best servants, the best enablers, the best helpers, and the best examples? What if a true leader resisted making it all about himself and made it all about his crew?

"Real leadership is rarely about giving orders. It is mostly about teaching, training, guiding, and shaping your crew. It is about being able to see what each crew member needs to succeed and then sets about helping them get it. We issue orders, sure, only when orders are a last resort. Orders resolve conflict and set priorities and manage emergencies. But if a captain is really doing his job by maximizing the ability of his crew, those conflicts and emergencies rarely arise.

"The measure of great leadership is not how necessary the

leader is to success, but how unnecessary. A truly great leader works himself out of a job by creating a team around him that can do it all without him. Great leaders are not threatened by strong followers; they are energized by them.

"Angie, you are all these things and more. Since leaving the service you have trained literally hundreds if not thousands to be effective in their jobs. You have a true service mentality and a heart to help. You don't have to become a leader; you are a leader. I've never been more confident of anything. You are just the person to head up this whole thing."

Sam Cogley walked in.

"Am I interrupting anything?"

"No, Sam. You're right on time. Angie and I were just finishing up our conversation."

Sam spread out the paperwork, and Angie and I set about signing it all.

The next morning Sam showed up at my holding cell bright and early.

"I just got word from the Coasties you'll be leaving tomorrow morning. They've had some trouble finding a way to transport you back to Earth. They can't spare one of their ships for the time to take you to Earth and then return, so they've contracted with the merchant marine to ship you like cargo. They were going to put you in a prison container in storage, but I got an injunction from the magistrate. I convinced him you weren't about to space yourself by stepping out an airlock unsuited just to escape going back to Earth. He agreed that as long as the ship was not in port, you did not have to be confined."

"I can be thankful for small things," I said.

"Look, Deke, I know we've discussed this, but I feel badly that I'm not going with you to defend you."

"It's OK, Sam. I get it. You can't just leave your practice to handle just one case...and one with a pretty low probability of a good outcome."

"It's not just that. It's that you've become a good and valued friend. This just isn't the way it should be. A friend takes care of a friend. It's eating me up, Deke."

"Sam, you gave it your best shot in court. Ahriman had the jury bought and paid for. Sein was in his pocket, too. And the pressure he brought to bear on the port authority to get a conviction was shameless. We had virtually no chance of success from the get-go. That wasn't your fault."

"My head knows all of that, Deke. But it doesn't make any difference to my heart. My heart knows this is wrong and 'wrong' should never win over right."

"The way things operate outside of our family, Sam, the ends justify the means. Use whatever tactics you have to use to get to the outcome you want. That's Ahriman's rules, that's the service's rules, that's life in general.

"But for us, we don't think about 'ends' and 'justifications'. We think only about the means. We don't even think the means justifies the ends. We just concentrate on the means: doing what is right at any given moment in any given situation. We don't concern ourselves with short-term goals, getting our way, or obtaining the objective we want. We think about the value of the present moment and the weight of the decisions we are making in that moment. Are they for us? Or are they for others? Are we giving or are we demanding?"

Sam already knew what I was saying. There was nothing to answer, nothing remaining to be said.

I saw him one more time that day. He came by the cell and dropped off a dozen or so of his antique books. He hated vids, but he loved to read. And his farewell gifts were some of his best.

In truth, I was not thrilled with Sam's news about me

going via a maritime service vessel. Even though it was probably a contract with the local Coastie command and whatever vessel was available in Euridian, I wondered if Ahriman knew about it. I also wondered if he did, would he himself assume command of the vessel? I could not think of a fate much worse.

When the next morning dawned, I was awake and prepared, waiting for my escort. The door opened, a couple of Coasties stepped in, and then, in full uniform, Draven Ahriman.

My heart sank.

CHAPTER 18 - **Journey Home**

"Give us a few minutes, boys," said Ahriman. Nodding, the Coasties stepped back outside. Ahriman didn't move for more than a minute, his eyes fixed on the door that had just closed. Then, slowly, he drew in his breath. I could see his shoulders rise. And then he let it out quickly in a heavy sigh. He turned and faced me fully, but his head was bowed. As he raised his eyes to look at me dead on, he was smiling.

"You're going away, Mr. Sandborn, for a long, long time. It's what the law does with criminals like you."

"I've appealed my case, Ahriman. Don't count your chickens before they're hatched."

"No, Mr. Sandborn, you've got nothing. You've got no fresh proof, no additional witnesses, and no other evidence than what you had in this trial. The appeals court likely will not even hear your appeal, but even if they do, it is a foregone conclusion what they'll decide.

"No, Mr. Sandborn, I've seen the last of you. Oh, you'll get out in about 20 years, but prison has a way of changing people. I won't be around. I'll retire, but I'll leave here knowing that if you were to make it back to this sector, it would be as a burned out hulk of the man you formerly were."

"So why are you here now, Ahriman?"

"Oh, to gloat mostly. You killed my son and then you attempted to ruin the business I labored my whole life to build. You hurt me, my family, and my business. Fortunately, when you are gone, the head will be cut from the snake and business will get back to normal.

"I will never get my son back, but at least I know that you will pay a price worse than death. You will have a living hell in prison and live out your days afterwards, despised and rejected. It does not answer my sorrow for losing Deegan, but it dulls the pain a bit.

"It's taken some time to get to you, Mr. Sandborn, but I have. I'm here to savor this moment. I'm here to taste my victory. I win. You lose."

Ahriman stepped to the door and spoke to the guards. "You can have him now. He's all yours."

Strangely, my heart was heavy, not for my plight, but for Ahriman's. Here was a man who had done nothing but dog my heels and make life difficult if not impossible...a man who had no kind thought for me...a man who would enable a lie that would cause me to go to prison wrongfully. By rights I should have been angry. I should have hated the very sight of him.

But as the echo of his words faded from my mind, all I felt was pity. I was saddened at him and for him. Had I had it in my power to do something nice for him, I would have done it...not to heap coals on him, but rather to answer the darkness and misery I could sense in him...to give him some one small positive thing amid all the ill.

Apparently getting revenge had consumed some larger part of his life since his son died and that was over now. I was, in his eyes, a defeated, vanquished foe. I was no longer worth his time, effort, or energy. I could sense the impending emptiness of his soul. Without an adversary, he would be rudderless.

He was at the pinnacle of his career, no doubt had all the money and possessions he'd ever wanted, and had left little to be accomplished with his remaining years. It was as if an invisible hand had pulled back the curtains of his soul and all that was there was emptiness…terrible, lonely emptiness. It reminded me of those eternities I had suffered in the chair. I shuddered involuntarily at the memory.

In that moment, the dichotomy was plain to me. The choice was to amass physical and monetary things as a hedge against the emptiness within, or to amass an inner wealth of meaning and generosity which made the external bulwarks unneeded. We had both made our choices. I would live with mine. I wondered if he was prepared to live with his, but I sensed not.

This was likely the last time I would ever see him. My last memory was of me walking unhand-cuffed and unfettered into the morning sun and him standing alone in the darkness of the jail that was meant for me.

The two guards and I walked toward the spaceport.

"Guys? Why didn't you handcuff me? I would bet standard procedure for prisoner transfer is at least handcuffs and possibly even shackles."

"Mr. Sandborn, you have your enemies, of that you well know. But you have family and friends, too. And some even in places unexpected." There was just the hint of a smile on the senior Coastie's face.

"Do I know you?" I asked.

"No, sir. I don't believe we've had the pleasure. My name is Lieutenant Miller. I believe you knew my brother."

"Bucky?" It was beyond hope.

"Yes, sir. He spoke highly of you the last several times we ran into each other. I don't know exactly what happened after he left the Rapacious and the merchant marine and joined you on the Revenant, but whatever it was, it was the best thing that ever happened to him. He became the big brother I always wished I'd had. He was still Bucky, but he was the best version of himself I'd ever known.

"Whatever you did for him or with him, sir, that's a debt I would gladly repay."

"What's your first name, Lieutenant?"

"Brougher, sir. But my family and friends call me 'Bowie'. I'd be pleased if you would, too, sir."

"Well, Bowie, that works for me as long as you call me Deke, and drop the sir."

"You got it, Deke. And may I introduce Petty Officer 1st Class Simpson. We're going to be your constant companions on this trip, it seems."

"Nice to meet you, Petty Officer 1st Class Simpson. Please call me Deke."

Simpson's grin was ear to ear. "Nice to meet you, Deke. You can call me Frank. My nickname is 'Knothole' but I think you should probably use 'Frank'."

I looked at Bowie. "Knothole?"

"You've perhaps noticed that Petty Officer Simpson is a bit on the tall and lanky side? During his basic training, the drill instructor told him he looked like his mother had pulled him through a knothole when he was born. The name sort of stuck."

He did sort of look that way. "Frank, your secret is safe with me."

"Thank you, sir. I know that you will be the heart and soul of discretion."

As we walked towards the spaceport, Bowie and Frank plied me with all sorts of questions about Bucky. I found out that Frank, Bucky, and Bowie had grown up together in the same neighborhood. They were both taken by the changes in Bucky and wanted to know what the deal was.

I tried to explain it as best I could without reference to Debris and the chair. They never saw Bucky after his turn in the chair, so they didn't know about that part of the experience. But Bucky had spent enough time around us he had definitely been influenced and begun the process of reversing the flow of his life from selfishness to selflessness.

I was, and still am, always amazed at how much of an impact that change has, not only on the individual, but on those around them. It always creates a sort of awe and curiosity. Bowie and Frank were no exceptions.

We were so engrossed in conversation, I almost didn't notice getting on the shuttle to the ship.

"Uh, Deke. There's been a slight change in plans. I believe you were told that you were being sent by commercial transport as the Coast Guard had no ship to spare."

"Yes, that was my understanding."

"Well, it seems as the senior officer in your security detail, I have some significant authority in arranging the terms and means of your transportation. I've learned as a Coastie that whatever authority they give you, it is on a use it or lose it basis. So I used it. I canceled the original transport in favor of another…uh…more suitable transport."

For the first time I looked up and out the view ports and there, as large as life, was the II.

"You've got to be kidding me." I could hardly contain my surprise and happiness.

"Nope. That's your transport. Fortunately, she was available for conscript."

I was speechless.

We docked and connected airlocks. When the panel turned all green, the airlock door swung open. I fully expected to see

Angie on the other side, but he was not.

"Brice?" I was dumbstruck. "What the hell are you doing here?"

"That's Captain Wilson to you, sir" said Brice with a mock air of authority. "I am in temporary command of the Revenant II. Allow me to present my First Officer, whom I think you know, Angelino Ariti."

"Angie!" I was, if possible, even more dumbstruck.

"As my first official duty as Captain of the Revenant II, I place myself, my crew, and my ship at your disposal, sir. Welcome aboard."

"Brice, how is this possible? Aren't you supposed to be on the Rapacious?"

"I am, or at least I was until this morning. Lieutenant Miller here canceled his contract and informed me the services of my ship were no longer required. He did, however, carelessly let slip the name of the alternative transport. I quickly put in for some overdue leave, packed, caught a shuttle, and commandeered this ship from its clearly ill-prepared crew." Brice was smiling.

"Ill prepared! Why you over stuffed, under qualified, over confident, under performing whelp! I'll have you know I sent Lieutenant Miller to the Rapacious with the intent to get you here. Ill prepared, my foot!" Angie was smiling, too.

"Well, I don't care," I said. "It's just great to have you both together again, even if it is to transport me to jail. This opportunity to be with you almost makes the trip worthwhile."

The back and forth went on for no little while as the crew prepared to get underway. My belongings arrived from the jail, the last thing we needed prior to leaving, and we started the journey back to Earth.

I was ambivalent. Part of me was thrilled to have this long haul back to earth with a crew I knew and two good friends.

Part of me was melancholy because I knew it was only a temporary reprieve until we got to Earth, where it would all come to an end once and for all.

It took a couple of days, but we all eventually fell into a shipboard routine. The crew was extremely competent, so there was little or nothing for me to do. There was even less for Miller and Simpson to do, but they were occupied working with the crew, learning things about commercial space travel that they never knew. It wasn't long before Miller was standing watches like the other officers and Simpson was enjoying stints in engineering and communications.

I was the totally unnecessary proverbial third wheel. Except for mealtimes and the occasional rare project I could help with, my time was my own. A day or two into the trip, I remembered the books that Sam Cogley had given me and broke them out.

It was quite the collection. Sam's tastes, if these books were representative, were wide ranging. There were a couple of philosophy books…Frankl was one author. There was an early adventure story by someone named Gray that involved horses and guns. I also found a biography of a General Grant, a fictional story of a spy named Bond, and several books on Earth history.

These were all antiques, books in the old-fashioned sense of bound pages with a spine and covers. They were old and delicate and had to be handled with care. But hidden away between two larger books (an Atlas from the 2200's and a history of art textbook) was a manuscript, stapled together of perhaps 50 pages printed double sided entitled "The Measure of a Man" by Simonds published in the early 2000's.

To some degree or other I had heard of most of the other books Sam had given me, but this one I had not. It had been downloaded and printed from the Library of Congress on

Earth.   Sam had clearly read it several times as I found copious notes of his in the margins in different colored inks. Originally, I thought the ink color was code for some sort of category of comment.   But I quickly realized they were not consistent. It had to have been that each time he'd read the manuscript, he'd used a different color ink to record his thoughts and comments.

There was a handwritten note on the cover page. "Deke, if you only read one, read this one. Sam". So I did.

It was exactly the book I needed to read.   It completely explained what the chair did to me and to every other person who sat in it. Yet it did so without ever mentioning the chair or even intimating that there was such a thing. Nevertheless, it was dead on in what it revealed to me.

I assumed the book was a classic of some sort, just not any classic I had ever heard of. But when I could get time on the comm's to check Earth data bases, there was no record of the book outside of the Library of Congress cloud.   Sam had found it, read it, and in typical Sam way, did not trust the cloud to ensure it was always available. He was Sam, so he downloaded and printed it out using good old-fashioned ink and good old-fashioned paper. I never saw Sam again, so I have no idea how he found this book. I'm just grateful he did and that he passed it on to me.

It was on my third or fourth time through the book that Angie stuck his head in the door and said, "We'll be landing on Debris in a couple of hours. Captain Wilson assumed you'd want to be on the bridge for that."

"Thanks, Angie. I do."

Early on in the trip we had all agreed to make the short cut that had originally brought us to Debris. It wasn't that we wanted to get to Earth quicker. It was an opportunity to go to Debris and actually spend a couple of days checking out the place.   When Miller and Simpson heard about Debris, the chair, and what it was to all of us, they were not only on board with the plan, but anxious to see the chair as well.

I had made the trip to Debris so many times I had lost count, but it never failed to give my heart a rush when this big shadow would suddenly reveal itself by the stars it blocked out. It was truly like a hole in space into which we were willingly flying.

The crew was experienced enough that the descent and landing were without incident, almost routine. We emerged on to the planet surface in the now familiar dark of night and felt again the brisk, crisp breeze. The tall grasses waved and rustled, raising a wall of background noise not unlike the oceans on earth.

It was both utterly alien and utterly familiar.

There was no morning to wait for, so the entire crew set off for the city as soon as we could be gathered. In all the times we had been there in the past, we had never seen evidence of anything that was the least bit concerning. This was a place that engendered calm and tranquility. There was no fear here.

Time was on our side this trip partly because we were taking a short cut to Earth that would cut days if not weeks off our passage. Even with this stop at Debris, we'd probably arrive well ahead of schedule. We spread out, determined to do a more thorough canvas of the city and its outskirts. In all the times past that I had been there, we always had pressing cargo contracts that we had to get back to as soon as possible. Our visits were sweet, but very, very short. We always went straight to the city center and straight back to the ship. But his time nothing was pressing but my appeal, and I was in no hurry to get on with that.

As we approached the first outbuildings, we split into two groups, one circling the city clockwise, the other counter-clockwise. The idea was every couple hundred meters to split off a couple of crew to move on a direct line toward the center of the city. Ultimately, the last of each party would complete the circle, meet on the far side of the city, and head in from there. In this way we hoped to compare notes in the central park and get an overall picture of the area.

When we finally met, we learned that there was nothing unusual about the area. There were, as you would expect, various sections of the city: residential, commercial, industrial, and a fair amount of open space. What was interesting was that there was no disarray or evidence of any kind of traumatic event anywhere. It was as though the entire population on one given day, packed up everything, swept and cleaned their homes and businesses, and simply left town.

Out of the entire crew, the only two who had never sat in the chair were Miller and Simpson, so the rest of the crew waited respectfully while Wilson, Ariti, and I accompanied them into the translucent building to the chair.

Miller deferred to Simpson, who went first. From an observer's perspective, the whole interaction took maybe three to four minutes of real time. Frank sat down and appeared to drift off to sleep. He did not twitch, move, or convey anything other than a restful catnap. When he awoke, he blinked and looked at the rest of us like we were specters or aliens. From his perspective, we had been standing there for eons. The last thing he expected was to return to the world exactly has he had left it. Like all the others, he was quiet and extremely preoccupied with his own thoughts as he got up and moved off to the side.

No one spoke. We all knew it was a solemn moment when you first awoke from the chair. Yes, it was like a collision of sorts: the worlds you had just experienced versus the world you left and returned to. Reorienting yourself was neither instant nor easy. It took time and effort. Realizing that an eternity had been compressed into minutes or possibly even seconds was, well, mind blowing. The concept was difficult enough to come to grips with, but the content was even more cumbersome. After all, you had an eternity of experiences that had come to you. You could not help but be changed in a moment.

Bowie, after witnessing it, sat down in the chair himself, only very gingerly...as though if he were gentle enough, he might assuage his anxiety. He, too, fell asleep in one state and awoke in another. Relative to the man Bowie woke up to be, he had fallen asleep as a boy. You couldn't help it. Having a lifetime plus an eternity crammed into your soul all at once matured you. You really were changed. You were not persuaded or convinced...you were changed. And you knew it.

As we waited respectfully for Bowie to collect himself, I found Brice and Angie looking at me intently.

Brice went first. "Deke, did you ever wonder what it would be like if you sat in the chair a second time?"

"No, not really. Why would I want to?"

"Well, you told me after my time in the chair that the chair simply took what you brought to it, amplified it, and played it back to you, allowing you to see the true nature of it all. That's why it was a different experience for each person who submits to it. It just occurred to me you, more than any of us, are a truly different person than when you sat in the chair the first time. If you sat in it again, you would bring an almost entirely new person to the chair. Your experience would be totally different the second time, it seems to me."

"I suppose so, Brice. You could be exactly right. In fact, you probably are. But I just don't think you're supposed to sit in it more than once. Once seems to me to be enough."

Angie chimed in. "I don't know about that, Deke. I've had this growing gut feeling that you're SUPPOSED to sit in it again. I can't explain it, and I wasn't going to say anything about it, but since Brice brought it up, it sort of confirms what I was feeling all along this trip. Deke, I think you're supposed to sit again.

"I don't think everyone should, like it is some sort of rule or law or such. I think it's just for you, Deke."

"Do you have anything to fear from the chair?" asked Brice.

"No. At least I don't think so. I know I respect it because of its power...like I respect a highly charged electrical wire. But, no, I don't fear it. I believe it is benign."

Brice and Angie fell silent but continued to look at me in that strange way. Deep in my core, I knew they were right. In fact, I realized I shared Angie's gut feeling and had for some time. When I got truly honest with myself, it was unavoidable.

I would sit in the chair again.

CHAPTER 19 - **Encounter**

"Greetings, Deacon Sandborn. We are glad you came back."

I had sat down in the chair and I was waiting for that sinking, sleeping feeling to come, but it didn't. Instead, I looked up and here was what could have been one of the statues from the square come to life.

"Guys! Guys, are you seeing this?" I looked to my left and right and Wilson, Ariti, Miller, and Simpson were there, but they were frozen. Not frozen, like in awe. No. Freeze frame frozen. Pause on the digital recording frozen. Frozen in the midst of a word or gesture.

"Please don't get up, Deacon. In fact, please sit quite still. You don't want to break contact with the chair."

I settled back and tried to sort this out in my mind.

"Who are you?" I asked. Seemed like a reasonable place to start.

"My name and the name of my people are probably unpronounceable, given the construction of your larynx. I could say them truly, but you wouldn't be able to repeat it. The closest approximation in your language would be this.

My people are called the Lancahwandahwahhani. My name is Cawfahfidahkah. That sounds harsh to my ears and I suppose yours, but it is the closest I can get. In our language, the middle of a word is the most important. The beginning and the ending merely modify or amplify it. Therefore, you can call me Fi."

He said this last in an almost birdlike way, "fee" with a momentarily extended "ee".

"How are you here, Fi?" Another reasonable question, I thought, since I had assumed the race was extinct.

"The same as you are here, Deacon. Like you, we can only be in one place at a time, and for now I am here as are you."

"But I have not seen you, nor have I seen any trace of you or your people in all the times I have been here. Do you live somewhere else and you have traveled here?"

"No, Deacon. We live here. We have always lived here. And as far as I can tell, we will always live here. You have not seen us because you cannot see us. Eternities ago we were as you are, living in corporeal bodies and moving so slowly upon the ground. But we changed and evolved and became as you see me now, a being of light."

He (I assumed it was a "he", I honestly couldn't tell) was right. He was s shimmering light, not a tangible entity.

"But shouldn't I have seen you before now? I can see you now."

"No, Deacon. Apart from the chair, you cannot see us. We are creatures of light. We vibrate at a speed which is beyond your senses. When you sit in the chair, your vibrations speed up to a speed close to ours. Did you think it not strange that you could experience eternities in what is to you mere minutes? It is because your vibrations became nearly as fast as ours.

"Even so, we have to slow down as slow as we can be in order for you to see us. Do we not appear shimmering and almost transparent to you? If I were to vibrate at my true speed, I would seem to disappear to you even though you remain sitting in the chair. At my slowest speed, if you were not in the chair, you would never be able to see me.

"We have watched you with great interest every time you have been here and followed you even into the sky for a short way. We are very curious about you and your kind, but mostly about you. You were not the first to sit in the chair, but you were the first of your kind, and the first of all other than ourselves to be changed. Before you sat, when you were cautiously walking and looking, we could see your vibrations and they were in such a manner that it was sucking all around you into you. All of your kind that we had seen before, vibrated in this manner, like little whirlpools.

"But after you sat in the chair, your vibrations changed. They vibrated in a new way such that they drew out from you what was in you, like a whirlpool in reverse, although such things do not exist in nature."

"It's true," I said. "When I got out of the chair, I felt as though I had been turned inside out. But what you describe is actually better, closer to what I actually felt."

I honestly don't remember all the conversation I had with Fi, partly because it went on for a very long time, and partly because I could never be sure if I was actually saying things out loud or merely thinking them telepathically. I was simultaneously more awake than I have ever been, yet in a dreamlike state.

Fi told me about his people and their evolution to beings of light. He talked about how in his world, light was like a substance. He and his kind breathed it, ate it, swam in it, and even flew with it. They lived primarily on Debris, although they were great explorers and often visited other planets.

They seemed to be reasonably aware of humans and our strengths and weaknesses. I suspect that they had been frequent visitors to Earth over the millennia, and some may have even taken up permanent residence there. Fi let certain things into the conversation which suggested a significant familiarity with our history and culture.

One thing I could not figure out, nor could I get a satisfactory answer from Fi, was to their lifespan. At the very least they were long lived. Their lives could be measured in thousands of our years. Or, it seemed at times, Fi was suggesting that they were immortal beings and lived without dying except by accident, but never of old age.

Their knowledge of just about everything was immense. Whether it was because they were immortal and therefore had the time to accumulate it, or they were just skilled teachers, passing the whole of their accumulated knowledge on from generation to generation...well, it didn't really matter.

"Fi?" I interrupted a monologue he was delivering on the centrality and necessity of meaning in life.

"Fi? Why are you here? Wait. I mean, why are you here with me now? I get the sense there is a reason for this meeting.

"The chair, in all the times I've seen it work in my people's lives, never wasted any effort or experience. Whether by design or quirk, the chair always has a reason or a purpose in everything it does. I realize I am here because the chair wants me here. I sense the same is true of you...you are here because the chair wants you here. So why, Fi? Why are we here?"

"The chair was never made for anyone other than the Lancahwandahwahhani. Others have sat in it...some to no effect...others to great effect, but not good and they often died. We have no way of knowing how the chair will effect any species other than our own. But to a person, when your people have sat in it, as near as we can tell, your experiences are very similar to ours.

"The chair was an invention of one of our greatest thinkers, Ahjehmajgiridmahpahn, Gi as you might call him. It was intended to be a sort of philosopher's stone. I use that term because I think it has great relevance in your culture. Gi lived in the millennia before we transcended to light and saw that our people had become lazy, self-involved, and greedy for things. Learning, science, the arts, all things of culture had given way to the pursuit of utility, profit, and gain. Instead of evolving, as a people, we were devolving.

"Somewhere along the line we had lost the key to life. We were dying, and we did not know it. But Gi did. He made the chair as a reset. He saw it as a way to take a Lancahwandahwahhani that sat in it and show him the ultimate value of his life. The principle was simple: if you knew the ultimate value of your life and saw that it was nothing, or even less than nothing, you'd change.

"What we had lost in our society was that sense of a meaning greater than our own lives. The chair brought us back to that. It became the touchstone we needed. It reminded us in the most impactful way possible, that death gives meaning to life. And it enabled us to see that meaning, or the lack of it. It enabled us to change.

"I think, Deacon, your people are where the Lancahwandahwahhani were when Gi made the chair. I think they have lost the meaning of life and have exchanged it for possessions. Am I not right?"

"Yes, Fi. That is exactly where we are. And are you saying the chair is our only hope?"

"No, Deacon, although that is a reasonable conclusion. The Lancahwandahwahhani were not as many as humans, and in those days we all lived here on Lancahwandahwah. As a race, you humans are growing in numbers faster than you could transport people here to Lancahwandahwah to sit in the chair. It would be a losing cause to rely on the chair. There is a better way if you are willing to hear it."

"I am, Fi." Was I? I wasn't sure, but his story had struck a chord with me and I wanted to hear it all the way through.

"It will require you to give up everything. Do you still want to hear it?"

"Fi, somehow I knew you were going to say that. I don't want to lie to you. In fact, I don't think I could, but I want you to know that I am willing to consider it."

"Fair enough. The Lancahwandahwahhani are students of time. We have studied time for as long as we have been Lancahwandahwahhani. While we are not time travelers ourselves, we have the science to look backwards and forwards in time.

"When we look at time, we note there are three types of time. First are the immutable periods. There exist in time certain periods where nothing can be changed from what history says happened during that time. What happened in those moments is so crucial to time, they cannot be changed. I do not mean we should not change them. I simply mean that so much of the future depends on what happened there is not enough temporal energy to make the change.

"The second is irrelevant time. It is time that is largely immaterial to the future. It can be changed, but to no actual effect because it is not in the least critical to the future. Time, in essence, doesn't care. Changes are easy but do not impact the timeline except for a brief period.

"The third we call time nodules. They are like buds on the timeline. They are times where something didn't happen but could have. So there are no future events to unmake or unravel. When a change is made in a time nodule, the ripple effect of change extends into the foreseeable future.

"When we look at your history, the history of your people, we note there is a point where they began to devolve into the morass of self involvement. It started in the 1960s in one generation and then multiplied itself into the next two generations until by the fourth generation it was dominant. However, there is a time nodule in the year 2020. We've identified a certain author who could have written a certain book that would have been very influential in reversing the flow of self indulgence. But he did not.

"We think you should go back to that time and convince him to write the book."

"Uh, OK. Um, time travel. Hm. A slight problem here… even you don't do that. At least that's what you said."

"No, we don't. We haven't needed to and so have spent no resources developing it. But that is not to say it can't be done. In fact, it can, and you and your crew are going to figure it out."

Time travel has been an interest of humankind forever. Traveling into the future is no big deal. It is a byproduct of faster than light travel and why time dampers were invented for our jump drives. I knew the mechanics of it at a high level, enough so I was aware of the dangers. The faster you go, the more time slows down for you relative to everyone else who isn't moving. So if it were possible to orbit the Earth at something close to the speed of light for a month, what would seem like thirty days to you would be centuries to those on Earth. When you landed, you'd be centuries into the future.

The problem is time travel is one way. You could travel into the future if you could go fast enough, but you couldn't go backwards into the past. So if you went forward in time into the future, you were stuck there and could not return.

Fi wanted me to go backwards in time several centuries. It had never been done because no one could overcome the limitation of speed. To go forward in time, you had to generate positive speed toward the speed of light.

Theoretically to go backward in time you'd have to do the opposite: generate negative speed...something less than zero speed...which is impossible.

"Fi, as far as I know, traveling backwards in time is impossible. The best minds of my race could never find a workaround for that barrier. I and my crew have no great technical background, so it is unlikely we are going to succeed where others much smarter and resourceful have failed."

"But you will, nonetheless. Your friend, Burkhardt, had nearly solved the problem. He had a flash of insight into it when he was calibrating the time dampers and jump drives. He made notes of his insights and brought those with him to your ship. They are still in the engineering logs even now."

My mouth hung agape. "He never said anything about it. He would have let everyone know if he had cracked that nut."

Fi countered. "He realized the potential of his insight, but he underestimated how close he was to a solution. To him it seemed a viable solution, but he expected it had some hidden flaw that would keep it from working out. So he put it away to work on another day. Unfortunately for him, that day did not come.

"Right now, you and I are in a time nodule. I can make you aware of the possibility of a solution, but I cannot solve it for you. The solution must come from you and your crew in the time stream. I can give you a clue: do not think of time as a linear construct. Nor should you think of it as a field. That is the limitation. Think of time as a dimension that can be changed relative to the other known dimensions. More than that, I cannot say."

If Fi was to be believed (and I had no reason not to believe him) he had just given me the key to time travel into the past, and possibly into the future as well without having to travel at or near the speed of light. Bucky's notes may not only have walked most of the way there in theory; knowing Bucky's penchant for tinkering, he may actually have outlined a feasible way to use the ship's drives to do it.

"Fi, why are you doing this? I am grateful, but I do not understand why you care about us."

"It is simple, Deacon. When Gi gave us the chair, he gave us the gift of generosity. As it changed us as individual Lancahwandahwahhani, it changed eventually the whole of the Lancahwandahwahhani. Instead of it being only an individual trait, it became a cultural trait of my people. As a race, we live to see other races reach their potential. It is, to use your scientific term, in our DNA. We cannot not do it.

"This is our gift to you, Deacon. And by you, I mean all of you...your race. Just as 2020 is a nodule, so is 2345. As you have your part to play in 2020, we have our part to play in 2345."

I wept because of the natural, instinctive gift of it all.

CHAPTER 20 - **A Matter of Time**

Looking back on it, we realized we should have seen it way before we did. But isn't that the case with all great scientific breakthroughs? Ultimately, it isn't the complicated, convoluted concepts that form the basis of new insight. It is the amazingly simple, palm to the forehead, should have been obvious ideas that burst into our minds.

The secret to time travel had been visible to us since the jump drive was first invented. It was the time damper. But we never saw the time damper as the technological lynch pin. It was just a convenient workaround for the problem of compressed time at light speed. Yeah. That's what we thought, so that's all we saw.

When I woke in the chair, I blurted out the whole story. It came out of me in a torrent of words, sometimes jumbled. I wanted to say everything before I forgot anything. There was lots of interrupting and asking me to repeat stuff because my stream-of-conscious was clearly on a different plane than what my listeners were capable of hearing. Eventually they got it.

"So let me get this straight," said Brice. "We're going to create a time machine that is going to allow you to go back in time, which, by the way, up to now has been considered impossible. You're going to...when?...2020, to somewhere in London? You're going to stop off and visit some guy you don't know and then hop back in the time machine to go further back to meet the same guy again? And in the meantime we're going to concoct some sort of story that you disappeared or died or escaped? Does that about sum it up?"

"Yeah," I said. "Those are the high points."

Brice looked at Bowie. "I'd give anything to have your brother with us right now. Did you inherit any of his engineering genes? Please tell me you did."

Bowie looked up. "No one could take Bucky's place in a plan like this. I have some basic aptitude. Our dad was a cracker jack engineer, and he taught us a lot. But Bucky was the star pupil, not me. I was always willing to help then, and I'm willing to help now, but I really don't know how much help I can be."

"Look, guys," I interrupted. "Fi was pretty definite that we would build whatever it is that we need to build to travel back in time. I've got to believe he wasn't just blowing smoke. If he says we build it, then you can bank on it, we build it."

Angie, ever the calm rationalist, brought us back to reality. "We don't need to worry about anything at this point. This speculation is a waste of energy. The first step, without which no further steps are possible, is to find Bucky's notes and read them. That's it. That's all. Then we'll know what the next step is. But not until we find and read his notes."

There was a moment of silence and then a chorus of mumbled agreement with the odd "I was going to say that" thrown in. Then we looked at each other and laughed at how quickly we got the cart before the horse. Good old Ariti. You couldn't argue with his logic.

We emerged from the building, gathered the rest of the crew, and headed back to the II. It didn't take long once we got there to access Bucky's files. And while there were a ton of them (Bucky was a prolific diarist), it wasn't hard finding the documents we needed. It helped that he had them all in a folder entitled "Time Travel."

Fi had said to make sure we did not think of time as a linear thing or even a field. We needed to think of it as a dimension. I wasn't entirely sure what that meant, but it made sense. If time was a dimension in a multi-dimensional construct, then it could be manipulated to the extent that every other dimension could be manipulated. In geometry, if you could manipulate height, you could also manipulate width and depth. If you thought of time in the very most fundamental way, it was a 4th dimension added to the three geometric ones.

We all knew that time was much more complex than that, that it was connected to gravity and acceleration and space in general. The traditional and dominant view of time was that it isn't really a dimension, even if we call it one. It is the measure of the movement of something through space. It is the tick of a clock or the vibration of a crystal. The traditional view of time was that it does not exist apart from that measure.

Fi was saying all that was wrong. That time is a dimension. That it exists in and of itself, just like any other physical dimension.

"Ok," said Brice. "I get all that. I just have no clue how to operationalize that."

Angie looked up from what he was reading. "Bucky struggled with that concept, too, from what I can see. So he quit trying to conceptualize it in his mind. He couldn't. He just held on to a really simple concept. Time dampers, according to him, are like clamps that keep the ship and its passengers from moving along the time dimension while the ship moves at incredible speeds along the physical dimensions of space. That's textbook, right?"

"Right," said Bowie. "Everyone that's taken even an introductory class in transport engineering knows the clamp analogy. But everybody was always taught that it was just that, an analogy, because understanding the real mechanics was far too complex for everyone other than genuine geniuses."

"But what if it isn't?" asked Angie. "That's the question Bucky asked. And he asked it because he realized that if you could calibrate the time dampers from 100% open...allowing time to flow/pass normally...to 100% closed...stopping time from passing at all...that you ought to be able to calibrate even further to reverse your direction in time. You wouldn't reverse time itself. You would simply move backwards on the timeline. You would move backwards past what had transpired in each of those past times.

"And he thought you could do it in a way that would dampen the effect on you of moving backwards in time, just the way the dampers worked when you were moving forwards. But that's as far as his thinking got." Angie sighed.

My mind had been struggling with this for a few hours now, and for a few days since we came back to the ship. I was missing something. It was something to do with seeing time as a dimension. But that was nothing new from the overly simplistic view. You knew about the three physical dimensions and time was simply a fourth added to them.

"WAIT!" I cried. "We've got this all backwards. When Fi told us to think of time as a dimension, we automatically went back to primitive thinking of time as the fourth dimension, added to the other three dimensions. Without realizing it, we were saying time was somehow less important than or dependent on the three physical dimensions. What if that's wrong? What if the primary dimension is time, movement? What if the other three dimensions are added to time, to make time visible? What if time itself is the key dimension without which none of the other dimensions exist?"

"Ok. You may be on to something there," said Brice. "But what does that give us?"

Frank had been very quiet, but he looked up and said something profound. "If time is the primary dimension, then we can move backwards by not moving at all."

We all looked at Frank, not sure whether he said something insanely brilliant or just insane. He wasn't talking about moving backwards in physical space because that has nothing to do with time. But what was he talking about?

"What if when the jump drives created that black hole that bends space, instead of moving to the far rim when it comes close, we just stay put? Think about this: we calibrate the dampers to keep time from moving forward as we move forward from one lip of the black hole to the other, and it stretches out again into conventional space. But you can't actually 'clamp down' and stop time. If you did, there's a logical impasse. If you stop time, time is stopped, and that means it freezes anyone in that state. If the dampers really stopped time, we'd be stuck in stopped time for eternity, frozen in that stopped moment and never able to exit it.

"No. The dampers must actually work to move us backward in time as we move forward, so we get to the other side at the same time we left the first side. It's like walking backwards on an escalator. You're moving, the escalator's moving, but the net effect is that you're standing still. The time dampers reverse time as time moves forward to keep us at zero. It just seems like time is 'frozen'. So what if we just stay still?"

Bowie gave out a low whistle. "Frank, I think you may have hit it. But could it be that simple? Just don't move? Just engage the jump drives to create the black hole and the time damper to do what they do, but just don't engage the actual drive that moves us?"

"It could be," said Brice. "The systems are so interlocked that it is virtually impossible for a vessel with jump drives to do what Frank describes unless we could uncouple them. The integration is virtually automatic and seamless between the particle ejectors, the dampers, and the drives themselves. Angie, did Bucky give any thought in that direction?"

"Yes, and no. He did some speculating about over-calibrating the dampers to move us back in time further than we moved forward, but the effect would have been very small from his perspective. So he seems to agree with Frank's assessment: the dampers could move us backward in time. But his thinking apparently didn't get to the point of actually realizing the potential of using the dampers alone for time travel, so he didn't speculate on the possibility of disconnecting the various parts."

Brice's brow was furrowed. "But it is possible. I know it. They can't be seamless, otherwise you couldn't calibrate the damper relative to the other two components. They must be able to be disconnected and operated independently. I think this is entirely doable. Let's do it!"

I hated to rain on their parade. "Guys, there just a slight problem here. Let's say this works. Let's say we figure out how to disengage the jump drives from the particle ejectors and the dampers. Let's say it all works and we don't just wink ourselves out of existence for whatever reason. Let's say we go all the way back to 2020 in however many jumps it takes. So here we are in 2020. You've dropped me off. How does the ship and crew get back to 2345?"

Silence.

"I see what you're saying, Deke," said Frank. "The dampers can take us backwards in time, but the technology does not exist to takes us forward through time again once we get there."

More silence.

"Well," said Brice. "I'm up for a road trip. Who wants to go to 2020 and live there?"

"Brice, cut it out. You can't take an entire crew back to 2020. First, most of the crew have families and significant others here and now. Second, we have no clue how to acculturate ourselves to the time. Third, there were diseases and viruses back then which were eradicated and which we have lost immunity to. We'd be biological sitting ducks. And those risks are just for starters. With a little effort, I can probably think of a dozen more."

He knew I was right. Everyone knew I was right. But how was I going to get back there if it was a one-way trip?

The light dawned.

"The Revenant! The Revenant! I can take the Revenant. That way the II can continue on its journey."

"No, you can't," said Angie. "The Revenant requires a crew of at least three."

"Well, actually it doesn't," said Brice. "That is if all you're going to do is sit in one spot in space and fire up your particle ejectors and time dampers. You wouldn't need a pilot or a navigator. You could do it all from engineering."

"Brice," said Angie. "I think you missed my point. He cannot do it alone."

"Oh. I see where this is going."

"So do I," I said. "Angie, get that thought right out of your head. Brice is right. I can do it alone. I'm prepared to run the risks of going back, including the not small risk of disease. But Fi told me about my going back, not anyone else, so I have confidence in my chances of survival. I don't have the same confidence about others. Besides, there is no real need for anyone to cast their lot with me and get stuck back in the early 2000s."

"Excuse me, Mr. Sandborn, but that's not your call to make." Angie's eyes were electric. "I think that's my call, sir. If I remember correctly, I am the rightful owner of the Revenant, and if you want to use it, you've got to get my permission. I can assure you, you may get my permission, but the Revenant is not going anywhere that I'm not going."

"Don't be silly, Angie. It's a one-way trip and you're needed here. Isn't that right, guys?"

I was met with a chorus of nay-sayers.

"Not really," said Brice.

"I don't need him," said Miller.

"I don't even know him, and I don't need him either," said Frank.

"But…"

"Oh, shut up, Deke," said Angie. "It's a done deal. I'm going."

"Well, it's not completely done," said Bowie. "I think I'll tag along, too. When I was in the chair, I got an inkling I was going to be given a life-changing choice. I believe this is it. Besides, you'll need a smarter engineer than what you make, Deke, to pull this deal off."

I heard Angie loud and clear. It hit my heart like a sledge hammer. I was willing to risk it all for what I thought was the right thing to do, but he was willing to risk it all for me. How could I not be moved by that? I had once pointed out that Angie never connected with the person he was serving, and here he was making the ultimate connection. Everything in my head was saying to insist that he could not go, but everything in my heart was gasping for breath at the magnitude of his commitment.

Bowie's offer was, if possible, even more impactful but in a different way. Without really knowing me, and only having sat in the chair a short time ago he was willing to commit to a simple idea: he was supposed to go…no reason other than it was what he was supposed to do. Such commitment was beyond even what I had done. For the second time I thought, how could I not be moved to say yes to that.

I thought about saying all of this to them and those around them, but decided this was not the time for flowery words or displays of emotions. This was the time for a gut check, an affirmation, and a handshake. I took a big inhale and….

"Well, gosh, I can't deny I'm not grateful for the company. OK. We'll go."

We shook hands all around and began to discuss next steps.

We tested out the damper idea on the way back to Euridian to pick up the Revenant to see how it worked. If we winked ourselves out of existence, no biggie. But no one really thought that would happen because of the confidence we had in Fi's instructions. He said we would solve the problem and we would go. That meant we would.

It was a very interesting trip back to Euridian. We tested what we started calling "the Damper Drive" several times on the way. It worked rough at first, but with tweaks and refinements we could effectively separate the jump drives, move successfully backwards in time, and actually calibrate how large a step back in time we could do. It all had to do with the size of the black hole the particle ejectors created. The larger the hole, the greater the backward movement in time. When we started with the smallest ejection that would create a navigable black hole, we found we only went back a few minutes. As we increased the size of the ejection we increased the time we traversed.

There turned out to be a exponential relationship between size and time. Initially, increases of size of the ejection had only small impacts on the amount of time we went back. But as the size of the injection increased, the impact it had on time became greater and greater. If the relationship held, there was a point at which relatively small increases in ejections would have relatively large temporal impacts.

This meant that we could have a precise control over our smaller jumps of a day or less. It also meant that in order to make big leaps, we wouldn't need huge amounts of matter and antimatter.

We became proficient enough in it we ended up getting to Euridian in time to see us leave the spaceport the first time for Debris and Earth.

When we showed up back at the spaceport, there was some surprise as they thought we had just left. We said we did leave, but we came back because we forgot something.

We had. The Revenant.

CHAPTER 21 - **Past Time**

Once aboard the Revenant, we figured we needed to not waste time engaging the damper drives until we got close to Earth. Disengaging the jump drives so that we could go back in time meant that we could not go forward in space. We had to remain still to travel back in time. But we needed to get to Earth so that when we went back in time, we were close to our target.

So we followed the II back past Debris and straight to earth. Of course we couldn't travel close together because our jump drives had to have clear space for quite a distance in order to work. We ended up arriving at the rendezvous point about a day and a half after the II. We "parked" ourselves in orbit around Titan. There was a risk we might be identified there, as it was home to a spaceport, but there was enough traffic going in and out, we figured we'd just blend in with the crowd.

Angie, Bowie, and I suited up and made the leap across the divide between the two ships for a last minute "skull session" before going the rest of the way to Earth. We would go separately, different routes, different speeds, leaving and arriving at different times.

"We need to come up with a cover story for the authorities on Earth to explain why you're not with us." Brice was right. Without that, they would arrest him and the entire crew for aiding and abetting an escape.

"It has to be something that also explains Bowie's absence. His absence will be noted, too. Ariti is another story. He's not a known entity, and he isn't expected anywhere, so no one will know that he's gone, too." Frank knew the story had to be good because he was the lone Coastie to be left, so he'd be "holding the bag" as far as Earth authorities were concerned.

Angie looked up. "How about a simple escape excuse? Deke escaped through the airlock and Bowie went after him, and they both died in space from the effects of a fight that ruptured both spacesuits."

It was a thought that had probably occurred to all of us. It was an obvious ploy and for that reason probably was not a good ruse.

"I don't think that'll work, Angie," I said. "You'd have collected the bodies in such a case, if only to recover the space suits and repair them. We wouldn't care about the bodies, but we'd have to get the suits so we could fix them for reuse. The authorities on Earth would expect that once we pulled them on board, we'd figure out a way to keep them intact. And we probably would have if that had been the cause of death."

Frank, ever the thoughtful one, looked at me with lips pursed. "What about explosive decompression? Suppose you and Miller were in or near an airlock and the airlock suddenly gave way into space. The two of you would be sucked out and would be dead within a minute or so, probably with ruptured lungs and swollen everything else.

We wouldn't have recovered your bodies in that case because we don't have the necessary medical facilities to store bodies."

Brice nodded. "That would work as far as explaining away the lack of bodies is concerned. But we don't have an exploded airlock. If the authorities questioned our story, and they likely will, at least by the Coasties, there's no damage."

"So we explode an airlock," said Frank. "The II has three. There's no significant impairment to the ship to lose one of them."

"We could do that," Miller said. "We'd just need to weaken the restraining bolts that secure the outer door, close the inner door, jack up the pressure in the airlock, and physics would take care of the rest. As long as we kept the inner door shut, that wouldn't impair the ship's operation. And I doubt, once the authorities saw the damage, they would look too closely. Yes. That could work."

"Brice, you're going to want to wait until we push off from this orbit on our last leg to Earth. When you get away from all this traffic, you can blow it and no one will see the explosion. You just want to make sure the entire crew knows the cover story and the necessary details of the who, what, where, when, and how," I said.

I doubted there would be much of an inquiry by local authorities on Earth, as we are a privately owned cargo ship and the "accident" supposedly happened in deep space off the principal trade routes. The Coast Guard would appoint an officer or two to investigate and might convene a board of inquiry, but it would be largely a formality since no Coastie vessel or crew were responsible for the accident. The maritime service would yawn. Even Ahriman, when he found out, would likely chalk it up to poor maintenance and accept the reports of my death as welcome news.

"Works for me," said Brice. He assigned one of the

engineering crew to start working on "aging" the airlock bolts.

We decided to have the Revenant leave orbit well before the II. That way, if anything went wrong with our backward "jumps", the II could still pick us up (assuming we were "pick-up-able") and we could rework the plan. We seriously doubted anyone would notice our jump back in time. There would be no explosion or flash of light or any other telltale sign. One second we'd be there, and the next second we'd be gone. If anyone was looking directly at us, they would likely just blink their eyes and shake their heads that they had thought there had been a ship there.

With the plan set and agreed to, there was no point in hanging around. After a somber goodbye, handshakes, and hugs all around, Angie, Bowie, and I suited up and "walked" back to the Revenant.

Within the hour we were underway toward Earth, where we would begin the first of a long series of damper jumps to take us back to 2020. Angie had done some archival research and determined that our clothing was such that it would most likely pass for early 21st century clothing.

Of course, we had no suitable medium of exchange or personal identification. That was something we'd have to figure out when we got there. I figured if we were just careful and didn't call attention to ourselves, the lack of identification would be a non-issue. Money would be the key need as nothing could be obtained without it. Our existing supplies would hold up for a while, but eventually we'd have to buy things.

I found these tactical concerns dominating my thoughts. It was funny that here we were, on the brink of a momentous event: time travel back in time and making contact with people in the past to impact the future, and I'm thinking about how difficult it is going to be to get a job and earn some money.

Within a week we arrived at a suitable distance from Earth to start the damper jumps. We were creating mini-black holes and so we couldn't get too close to Earth or anything substantial for that matter. We parked, did the decoupling routine to deactivate the navigation elements of the jump drives, and did a small jump that would take us back about 20 minutes.

It worked fine. Our test was that we expected to see us heading toward us as we were still in the same place, just a slightly earlier time. We knew we'd have to move quickly if it worked to keep from ramming ourselves. We jumped, there the earlier us was, we sped up to maximum sub-light speed to put enough distance between us, and when safely distant, jumped again, only this time much further back in time.

Thus began a prolonged series of jumps, taking us ever further back in time. Up to now we'd only been jumping in small increments of time. We'd used the navigational system to guesstimate the amount of time we'd gone back in time. Star navigation software has a computational feature that allows for minute changes in star positions due to time. When we jumped backwards in small increments, we'd get an error in our navigational output. But if we adjusted the ship's chronometers back slowly enough, we'd hit a time when the nav system would show our position as correct. It was laborious to do that by hand, but it was the best option we had for small jumps.

We could have taken two or three large jumps, but we were concerned we would overshoot our mark. We had a specific date and time that Fi had given us and if we overshot that, we would be stuck in time waiting for the timeline to pass before we could act. So our jumps started somewhat large and then progressively got smaller and smaller as we got closer and closer to the target time.

Once we started taking jumps of more than an hour or two, we could no longer use the nav system to figure out the exact time. Being closer to Earth we were able to use radio and TV signals to determine months, days, and years. We'd jump and then use the communications gear to scan the radio frequencies for programming and the time checks that are routine with them.

We figured we needed to get to London at least a day early, possibly a few more, to scout out the necessary routes and landmarks. As it turned out, Bowie's engineering, Angie's navigation, and my time checks put us in far Earth orbit 48 hours early.

The Revenant was small enough that we did not have any on board shuttles. We needed to land somewhere in or within walking distance of London without being noticed. This was no small feat for one of the largest, most populated urban areas in the world.

Once again, Angie had done his homework and found an area large enough and even abandoned where we could land and be secure: Hornsey Wood Reservoir under Finsbury Park. It is an underground man-made lake of sorts, that by 2020 had been abandoned for so many years that most of London was unaware of it. Angie had uncovered some old city planning documents that disclosed a remote entrance in a wooded area that was large enough to navigate the Revenant through. It had been a construction access tunnel that had long been forgotten along with the reservoir itself.

The location was perfect. It was six miles from Victoria Station, but less than that to the hotel where Simonds was staying. We needed to do some planning to make it work as we had to make a second jump back two weeks to meet him at Victoria Station after I met Simonds at his hotel.

The plan was that the Revenant would land in a wooded

area near Finsbury Park and drop me off the night before meeting Simonds at his hotel. The meeting had historical significance as far as the Lancahwandahwahhani were concerned, and they had found out he would stay at the Thistle Piccadilly Hotel, not far from the Church of England headquarters. I would arrive early in the morning, spend the day with him, and then head back to the Revenant.

That would be the easy meeting. It would be the second time he had seen me, so I would be familiar to him and the discussion would flow freely. In his timeline, he had already met me at Victoria Station, but this was my first time in meeting him. I wondered how that would work out. As it turned out, just fine.

After that meeting, which would last all day and into the early evening, I would head back to the woods where the Revenant would land again and pick me up. From there, we'd navigate a safe distance from Earth, then jump back the two weeks. We'd pilot the Revenant into Hornsey the night before my meeting in Victoria Station. There the Revenant would stay, presumably forever, as we were not going back in time any further. We'd use it for a home base for the two weeks between the Victoria Station meeting until after the meeting at his hotel. At that point, we would be caught up with ourselves. I'd go back to Simonds' hotel and let him know we were "stuck" in 2020, and ask for any advice or help he might have to give. We hoped he would help us solve the identification, housing, vaccination, and employment problems we faced.

With or without his help, though, we would become citizens of the 21st century.

I don't know what I was expecting the morning I knocked on the door to room 21C. I guess in my mind I had a stereotype of an author...a tweedy sort of guy, short, bespectacled, reserved, bookish. What greeted me was a six foot tall, slightly balding man who had a wide smile and an even wider welcome. He was dressed in jeans and a turtleneck, barefooted, with a sense of a man much younger than his actual age. His sense of humor was evident from the first, and you just got the feeling that even if he didn't understand everything you were saying, he was at least listening. He seemed intelligent and quick, but went out of his way to make you feel comfortable and accepted.

I liked him immediately. He was a man who had no guile. You got the sense even without evidence, this was a man you could trust. And I did. Instantly.[9]

After the exchange of a few pleasantries, we got down to business.

"I know this is your first time meeting me, so please forgive me my enthusiasm in greeting you. I've spent two weeks alternately excited about and dreading this meeting. I didn't know until I got the paper this morning how it was going to turn out. And let me tell you, when I looked at the paper you gave me two weeks ago as compared to the one left at my door this morning, I got quite giddy. I'm sure my enthusiasm must have taken you by surprise. I hope I didn't make you feel uncomfortable."

"No, your enthusiasm didn't make me feel uncomfortable. The whole idea of meeting you the first time in a time 325 years before my own time made me more than uncomfortable enough. I honestly did not know what to expect, Mr. Simonds. So your enthusiasm and positive acceptance actually made me feel more comfortable."

---

[9] You realize, I'm sure, that I am writing this about myself. It sounds very self serving and egotistical, I know. But you should also realize it is not my view of me. My view is much more irascible and obviously flawed. But he insisted I write it from his perspective without editing it. This was his introduction to his first 21st century denizen.

"Housekeeping issue. Please call me Skip. It is a childhood nickname I could never shake. I'd say my friends call me that, but in truth everyone calls me that. So you should, too."

"Thanks, Skip. Did I tell you my name two weeks ago?"

"Yes, Deke, you did. I'm still wrapping my brain around this whole time travel thing. Given that this is your first time meeting me, as I understand it, you are sort of 'on your way' back to two weeks ago. You haven't been there yet, right? I would have thought you would have gone there first."

"No. Unfortunately, time travel is still in its infancy. In fact, my crew and I are the first, ever. We solved the problem of going back in time, something that was thought to be theoretically impossible. However, while going forward in time, traveling into the future, is theoretically possible and has been for centuries, the practical application of it has never been developed. In fact, barring some new technology from my time or later, it does not ever look like the practical limitations will get solved, even though theoretically they are solvable."

Skip looked pensive. "I'm no scientist, Deke, but if that means you have to go here first and then to two weeks ago because you can't travel forward in time, doesn't that also mean once you get back to two weeks ago, unless you want to go further back, you're stuck there experiencing time in the normal way?"

"Unfortunately, yes. Once we jump back two more weeks, we're essentially done."

"And that means you won't be able to get back to the future." Skip let out a low whistle. "Deke, I am so sorry you're stuck here. I had thought, if it turned out you were a time traveler, that you could go pretty much anywhere and any time you wanted. But this was a one-way trip, wasn't it?"

"Yes, sir."

"You just didn't do this on a whim. This is serious business to you. You were willing to separate from family and friends forever and sacrifice your life and future for this."

I couldn't answer him. I just looked down at my feet. Silence filled the room.

"Well, damn, son. If it's that important, we better get to it."

CHAPTER 22 - **Closing the Loop**

I spent the rest of the day working with Skip on the project, and we roughed out the opening chapter of the manuscript. There was some discussion about what kind of book to make it. We both agreed it needed to be an allegory rather than a non-fiction retelling of my life from the chair on, complete with time travel. Call it a long-standing habit that Angie and I had worked out originally on the Rapacious to avoid the appearance of insanity. Skip agreed. There didn't seem to be anything to be gained by trying to convince people it was a true story and completely destroying what reputation Skip had as an author and public speaker.

Initially, I thought a simple novel set in the current time would suffice. I see now I was wrong. There were just too many elements of the story that would have been impossible to set in the 21st century. Skip has always been a fan of science fiction, and in fact had written a short juvenile science fiction book years before. He'd wanted to try his hand at something more meaty and adult-oriented since then.

I immediately realized the value of approaching it this way.

The audience would receive it as a fiction, specifically science fiction with all the trappings, only what we were really doing was writing a true historical non-fiction book. We could tell the truth the exact way it happened without running the risk of being thought crazy.

But then Skip took it even further and suggested we set the story up as if it really was non-fiction, complete with asides to the reader letting them in on the truth. And that was where the idea for the opening chapter of the manuscript came from. It was the critical letter to "Dear Reader" that was like a break in character in a play where the actor steps out of character and says something directly to the audience. Skip felt it would be just cheeky enough to add to the panache of the story, but that a small core of readers might see through that and understand the truth.

It made sense. The allegory would still stand. The lesson of the chair would be published and read and hopefully impact people whether they read the story as allegory or truth. And for those who realized, as improbable as it seemed, that it was a true story.... Well, the seeds of a "family" would begin to be sown some 325 years earlier that it otherwise would have happened.

It took less than an hour for Simonds to rough out the first draft of that opening chapter. He wrote the bulk of it because for him; it had already happened. He just described it as it took place. For me, it was a genuine work of fiction because it described a meeting that in my timeline hadn't happened yet. But it was also a work of prediction, because it was describing something that would happen. It was odd to read it, realizing I was going to go back in time and say stuff, supposedly spontaneously, that in Skip's timeline was already said, and therefore, concrete history.

It took some effort to get over the feeling of anxiety that I was going to go back in time to that meeting and somehow mess it up.   To me, the manuscript was a script I had to memorize almost word for word. But Skip pointed out that I couldn't mess it up, because I hadn't messed it up. Oddly, that bit of illogic made me feel better. I would say what he remembered I said because it would be the most natural thing for me to say when I said it.

I spent the rest of the day telling Skip my history from the chair onward.   He took copious notes and even recorded some of it on his computer, the quaint thing that it was. I had read about them, but never seen one outside of a picture. It was huge by my standards, and bulky and unwieldy in the way information had to be entered by hand. Skip assured me it was actually smaller than most of the other models available, and quite advanced. I did not have the heart to tell him how antiquated it really was.

By the end of the day, sometime close to midnight, I had to cut the story off and leave us somewhere right after we had "purchased" the Revenant II. I had to meet Angie and Bowie and head back to the meeting two weeks earlier at Victoria Station.

"I'll come back tomorrow morning and we'll pick up where we left off."

"Wait. What?"

"I'll come back tomorrow morning and we'll pick up where we left off.   You may have to remind me where we left off because for me, it will be two weeks and a day between tonight and tomorrow.. I'm going back in time with no way to get back to right now other than the 'old-fashioned' way of just letting time pass.   I'm going to have to wait on the Revenant from then until tomorrow."

Skip sighed. "That just seems wrong to have you cooling your heels for two weeks.   We should be able to use that time."

I chuckled. "Yes, except you weren't sure I wasn't a...what did you call me…a grifter? You weren't sure until today's paper came out. So I wouldn't have been welcomed before today."

"Oh, my god! I just realized. You're actually sitting in Hornsey Wood Reservoir right now!"

I couldn't help but chuckle again. "You know, Skip. I didn't realize that either until you just said it. Now that's funny."

Taking my good-by, I left, promising to return bright and early the next day. I was heading back to Finsbury when the thought occurred to me I knew where the entrance to Hornsey was, and I could easily just go in and see my future self who had gone in their two weeks ago and who would be waiting for me to leave this day. I could have, but I decided not to. I really didn't know what would happen if two versions of me got too close to each other. Besides, maybe I was outside the Thistle right now, somewhere in the shadows, watching me leave. Knowing me, I probably was. I waved, in case I was right. I heard an answering whistle. Was that me? I decided the best course was just to keep walking.

It was late, but I retraced my steps back to where we had landed the evening before in Finsbury Park. The ship was there, as planned. I boarded, and we took off as quickly as possible.

It wasn't long before we were far enough out to begin the relatively small steps we needed to go back two weeks. We took it in tiny bites, going only a few days each jump. In between jumps we had to pause and listen for time stamps on radio signals from Earth. The data on the relationship between size of the particulates ejected and the length of negative time we experienced was growing each jump. We were getting better and better at setting a target time and hitting within an hour or two of either side of it.

Again, we knew we needed to be a day or two early to allow for any unexpected contingencies. Our last jump took us just shy of 36 hours before I was to meet Skip in Victoria Station. It was our first shot at finding the entrance to Hornsey Wood Reservoir and as expected it was long overgrown and almost impossible to find. There were multiple entrances through utility hole covers near and in Finsbury Park, but the maintenance tunnel had not been used since the late 1800s and so had been not only abandoned, but purposely allowed to become almost indistinguishable from the surrounding landscape.

We landed in as dense a landscape as we could find, about where we had/would land two weeks from now on our way back. It took several hours with the diagrams Angie had located to find the entrance, and then several more hours to clear a path in such a way that it could be re-covered after we had flown the Revenant in. It would do no good to hide it and leave a path as wide as Broadway pointing toward it. There were still access points leading to the park above, but the reservoir was huge and we found a section that was somewhat separated from the main cavernous area, an unlikely spot for anyone to look who was exploring the underground, not that this was even allowed anymore.

Once the Revenant was in and we had rearranged the plant growth to look as natural as possible, we all breathed a sigh of relief. The Revenant had come to its ultimate resting place.

After a quick meal and a change of clothes to the most innocuous ones I had, I left the ship and exited the reservoir through one of the access points. I knew where Skip was staying, and it was more or less on a line in the general direction of Victoria Station. Skip had given me enough money that I could have taken the Tube, but the night was clear and brisk and I decided to walk. I covered the distance in roughly 2 hours, using the directions Skip had given me.

It was early morning when I arrived the first time, the day before I was to meet Skip. I walked through the station and stopped at the bakery where we would meet the next day, had black tea and a local pastry…something called a Chelsea bun. It was hot and sweet and very sticky. I sat and watched the commuters, old and young, male and female, and even some whose gender I could not determine. It was a collection of motley colors and styles and fashions. I was struck by how much shorter these people were compared to the people of my day, on average six or more inches. I needed to remember that I might be conspicuous in this period, if only because of my height.

I listened to the conversations. Mostly, I understood the snippets I overheard. There were words that were strange to me. For example, I heard several times that things that couldn't possibly give off light were "brilliant." There was a complete indecipherable word "bollocks" which seemed to be applied to a lot of distasteful things. And perhaps most puzzling of all, I heard a couple of times that a few seemingly unrelated people who walked by me at different times shared an uncle named "Bob."

As I finished my bun and tea, a young couple came up and asked if they could sit at my table as all the others were taken. I welcomed them and they sat down, but they did not talk or engage. They just sat and looked intensely at two hand-held devices waiting for what they called "a signal." Apparently it never came, as I grew tired of waiting to engage them and took my leave.

I recalled later that one thing I was to tell Skip was that there was no signal in the Tube and that's why his phone hadn't rung. The whole concept puzzled me. I knew about radio signals, but this "signal" seemed to be different, almost like telepathy. But perhaps Skip's signal and what these young people were looking for was the same. Perhaps those were phones…whatever phones are.

With space travel, especially superluminal travel, and the colonization of larger and larger areas of space, the social and political doings on Earth had become less of a focus of civilization. By 2345 more than half the human beings alive lived and or worked full time in space. When that tipping point had been reached a few generations before, the view of Earth as a hub in social, monetary, political, and governmental terms began to erode. What happened on Earth was still news, but not the only news, and less and less often the really important news.

As I left Victoria Station, I picked up a copy of a local newspaper, different from the one Skip had given me. It was the Daily Mail. The stories were predominantly British, then the Commonwealth and individual European nations, and then American. But they were stories of national interest at the highest level, and intensely local as one read past the first several pages.

There were very few international stories, or stories of things that had implications for the Earth in general or even large groups of nations. In neither the reader nor the publisher, there seemed to be no consciousness of a sense of global interest. All was intensely national.

In 2345, I guess globalism had replaced nationalism, because one rarely read stories in the electronic versions of newspapers on the first few screens about national concerns. They reported things in terms of worlds, not nations. National stuff was buried deep in the screens and rarely interesting to anyone except those who lived in those nations. Matters were global.

I worked my way back to the ship by evening, having taken a walking tour of the palaces and gardens scattered along the way. This new home of 2020 was going to take some getting used to. I talked with Angie and Bowie about my day and tried to make them understand how our horizons would from this point on be severely limited. It would come as a shock to all of us suddenly to be confined to a single planet. It would come as a bigger shock to realize we were largely confined to a single nation.

The next morning I met Skip at the bake shop in Victoria Station. It was weird to be saying almost verbatim what he told me I was going to say, and yet feeling like each word and phrase was spontaneous and original. How could both those things be true simultaneously? Clearly they should not. They should have been mutually exclusive. But they were not.

When the meeting was over, I returned directly to the Revenant and worked with Angie and Bowie in the decommissioning process. We had decided to not only render the ship unusable, but also to dismantle any technology that wasn't already present in 2020.

Once dismantled, those pieces had to be disposed of in such a way so as to never be assembled again. It was an enormous job. There was all the obvious stuff and lots of the dials and controls that were visible. But there was also equipment in the Revenant's guts that had to be "dug out" and taken apart.

Each night, the three of us went out well after midnight and took the day's output to be disposed of. We found trash cans and dumpsters in the surrounding areas, but we decided to only put a few parts in each, and only parts that were taken from different pieces of equipment. That way, even if someone found the parts, no one could reassemble them.

Each night we went to a unique area and never used the same area twice, a further insurance that pieces could not be reassembled. We only worked long enough each day to generate the most parts that could successfully be thrown away each night. That meant that most days we only worked on actual dismantling efforts for a few hours. At that rate it was going to take over two weeks, not so much for the deconstruction, but to ensure our disposal process remained undetected.

When it was day and we weren't working, we listened to radio broadcasts to try to assimilate a working knowledge of the culture while we were still in hiding. The programming was mostly music, and very old fashioned by our standards. We did find some all news signals that we would listen to, but you could only listen to them for so long. They seemed to blur the lines between news and commentary about the news. The stations reported on largely the same stories, but where one seemed to report an item as being positive, another reported it as being negative. We quickly tired of what we easily perceived as partisanship.

Whenever we could exit Hornsey safely, we would go out and walk about a bit. It was rare we all went out together, but occasionally we did. At those times we might go to what the locals called a pub and quickly learned that the beverage of choice was beer. Of course we had beer in our time, but it was a far cry from this stuff. Ours was weak and watery. This was heady and flavorful. Each of us quickly defined our "favorite" and ordered that repeatedly.

When we went out individually, it was often just to scout out the areas around Finsbury Park and learn what we could of the social practices of the day. We always tried to wear different clothes on successive days so that we did not become "familiar" to anyone. We didn't have many clothes, and we often had to swap clothes to keep our appearances shifting. That worked fine for Bowie and me, but Angie being short was at a decided disadvantage.

By the time the two weeks had passed after our last jump into the past, we were all tired of being cooped up by day. On the day before we knew we were going to be landing to drop me off to see Skip for the first time, we all decided to exit the Revenant and station ourselves in the woods around the landing site, primarily to act as a sort of distraction if anyone noticed a spaceship landing in the woods. But there was definitely the excitement of getting to see ourselves in action. We'd all seen vids of ourselves, but to see yourself in real life was a whole barrel of different. It was startling and difficult to describe thereafter.

Of course none of us saw any locals that night, so there was no one to distract. As soon as the previous me disappeared on my walkabout, we all retired back to the Revenant to wait out the rest of our confinement.

The next evening we all decided to walk the four miles to the hotel where I was meeting with Skip and to follow me back to the landing site, again to act as security. When I appeared at the front of the hotel, I saw myself stop and look around, and then wave. I thought how stupid that looked, and then Bowie put his fingers in his mouth and whistled. Angie and I punched and shushed him, but we were all giggling, too. We were like teenagers anticipating a first date. Life was about to begin again for us, only in a whole new time on a truly blank sheet of paper where we could literally be anyone we wanted to be.

We followed me back to the landing site, watched the Revenant descend and then ascend after picking me up, and then we all went back to our current Revenant and slept soundly.

The next morning, I left relatively early to head back to Skip's hotel reminding myself that I had just been there yesterday even though for the present day me it had been two weeks plus a day. I was ready to start work in earnest on the book. When I arrived at the Thistle Piccadilly, Skip was waiting and similarly ready to jump into the project.

We worked together so well; me picking up where I left off

in the story, Skip taking notes and asking questions, we lost all track of time. It was late afternoon when we took our first actual break. Like anybody laboring intensely, we both stood up and stretched. Seemingly on cue, there was a knock on the door.

"Are you expecting anyone? Perhaps Angie or Bowie? I'm not."

"No. They're still in the decommissioning process and won't be finished until the end of the week."

Simonds walked to the door, opened it, and an older, swarthy gentleman stood in the hall.

"Yes?" said Simonds, seeing it wasn't anyone he knew or any of the hotel staff. "Can I help you?"

"I'm looking for Deacon Sandborn. Is he here?"

Hearing my name, I looked up. Instantly, my heart froze in disbelief. I couldn't speak, but my mouth formed the word soundlessly.

"Ahriman!"

CHAPTER 23 - **Wrestling in Time**

"May I come in?"

Dubiously Skip looked at Deke who nodded faint assent.

"Thank you. I wasn't sure you would allow me in since I came here to kill you...probably both of you if need be." Ahriman took off his coat. It was an expensive one, the Gieves & Hawkes label visible as he laid it on the bed.

"And?" asked Simonds nonchalantly. I had to admire his cool at this point.

"And I was totally committed to the project until a few weeks ago. Now...well, let's just say I have seen the error of my ways. Gentlemen, I repent. I am your humble servant."

First, the last person I expected to see at the hotel room door was Ahriman. Second, the last thing I expected to experience from an Ahriman who showed up literally out of nowhere was civility. And third, the last thing I expected to hear from a civil Ahriman who showed up literally out of nowhere was an apology...and an offer of service. I don't think I could have spoken even if I could have thought of something to say. And I definitely couldn't think of a single thing.

He sat down in one of the overstuffed chairs, gently smoothed out his pants, and leaned back with an arm thrown over the back of the chair. He had the air of a gentleman, but it only went skin deep. His eyes bespoke a flame of avarice burning fiercely within. As long as you didn't look at his eyes though, his demeanor was almost 'to the manor born.' Perhaps it was his years of military discipline, or perhaps he had become used to the wealth he had amassed and assumed the advantages it conveyed as his due. He may have said he came as a humble servant, but the reality was anything but.

I finally found my tongue. "I suppose you think we should thank you for not killing us." My sarcasm was barely in check. As near as I could tell, he had no weapon, and I was more than a physical match for him, both in size and age.

"No, of course not. I realize my appearing here is a shock to you. After all, time travel is certainly not common knowledge. In fact, until you did it, it wasn't even thought possible except for traveling into the future."

"People back home know about it?" I asked.

"Of course not! And I doubt they ever will, elsewise the past would be littered with one-way travelers from the future. Clearly it is not.

"No, I found out about it because you told me enough for me to figure it out."

I was shocked. "I most certainly did not!"

"Well, not directly, I'll grant you," Ahriman said. "But it was you, and you, too, Mr. Simonds."

"I've never seen you before today, let alone talked to you. And I've known about time travel for two weeks…and only been convinced of it since yesterday morning. So, no, I did not," Skip said.

"Ah, but you both did. But perhaps I am getting ahead of myself. Let me start at the beginning…way back in 2345. I had just found out about your death, Deke. The story came back to me through a back channel of former shipmates back in Earth Maritime Headquarters. They knew I would want to know. I think they thought I would be glad you were dead instead of being in prison.

"But the news hit me quite differently. I dug into it. And the more I dug into it, the more it became apparent that your death was at best a suicide, but more likely a subterfuge. Yes, I was suspicious there was some deceit. When I learned your guards had booked passage on your own ship, I knew something was wrong. When I learned you had returned to pick up a second ship literally minutes after leaving for Earth, I was sure there was a plan of some sort.

"So I started with the assumption you were still alive somewhere. As soon as I made that assumption, other things about your death began to make sense. Bucky Miller's brother was your guard and died with you? I think not. Ariti was there when you left Euridian, but not when the ship arrived on Earth? Beyond curious. A blown airlock that just happened to give way without warning while you and Miller were actually in the airlock? Too many coincidences to it to be the truth.

"So if you weren't spaced, where were you? Most likely you would have gone to some place that was familiar to you…some childhood haunt…some remembered vacation spot…family, close or distant…even just an ocean isle you might have always dreamed of going to. You know what they say: Everyone has to be somewhere.

"I started an exhaustive search of the nets for anything and everything I could find out about you that might give me a clue to where you might be. I looked at old transportation records to see where you had traveled on Earth. I looked at relatives of yours, especially those a bit removed from you in order to send teams to check those locations for sign of you.

"I looked at school year books and academy admission records and even did some research on your ancestry. I hired a private detective to look into elements of your life which might not be visible to me as a matter of public record. He looked for criminal records, financial histories, and known associates. He built a timeline of your life complete with a level of detail I thought impossible. Between it all, I turned up a whole host of potential locations for you to be hiding in plain sight. And you were in none of them.

"You had seemingly vanished into the space your airlock was supposed to have drawn you into."

Ahriman paused.

"But then, after I had run down every lead, sent sleuths to every location, and questioned every significant relation and friend...when I was about to give up and admit I had been wrong and you truly were spaced...my detective brought me a somewhat improbable piece of information that didn't seem to fit into any rubric I had constructed. There was this book, published in the early 21st century that had, as its main character, a Deacon Sandborn.

"I got a copy and read it, and there in black and white was the whole story, laid out in enough detail that I could piece together all the confusing pieces I already had, and with sufficient information to make assumptions about the pieces I didn't have.

Ahriman removed his arm from the back of the chair and put both elbows on his knees as he leaned forward. "Time travel...and backward time travel at that...who would have even guessed?"

I looked at Skip as he looked at me and we shared that one moment of insight in a heel of the hand to the forehead realization. By deciding to write the book without disguising the actual events and characters, we had given away the secret of time travel and my plan to change history. As we were writing the book, future events were slowly but inexorably beginning to change. Just our intention to write it this way had already sent ripples through time to enable some form of the finished book to pop into existence in 2345. As we completed more and more of the book, the ripples would become deeper and more ingrained.

Ahriman had, in that precise moment of change that occurred in the future as we in the present planned and wrote, found a copy of the book as it existed but before it became famous and a true agency for change. Apparently time ripples unfolded in the future at the same speed as we created them in the past. We had the intention to finish and were making the effort to finish, but the book was still an incomplete work in progress in our time. Being in a time nodule like Fi had described apparently conferred on us the power to change the future by an event that was unfolding, rather than all at once. We were free agents in that unfolding and could have decided to stop writing the book at any time, with the results of that decision halting any further potential change that might have happened had we completed the book.

It was too late to stop now, of course. Ahriman had, by the sheer luck of timing, found enough of the book as it would be if we quit writing right where we were, to figure out how to end up back in 2020. However, the book was not yet influential, and it needed to be. We could not right the wrong of Ahriman's discovery, but we could mitigate it by finishing the book and letting those ripples flow forward and change the future for the good.

In my logical mind, I guess I had always assumed that the future would be changed instantly. I was wrong. The timeline was shifted and moved incrementally just as we were changing the past we were living in incrementally through writing a book that would not otherwise have existed.

"Who would have guessed? Well, you apparently," Skip replied. "But none of this explains your change of heart towards Deke. In fact, I find it unlikely that it would have had that impact at all. It is more likely it would have intensified your dislike for him in that he escaped the doom you had arranged for him."

"Oh, it did. It did, indeed. I was beside myself with fury." Ahriman leaned back again and assumed an air of command, no doubt honed through years as a senior officer in the maritime services. In fact, his demeanor was almost professorial, as though he were preparing to explain something obvious to an ignorant or naive student.

"My anger motivated me to risk developing my version of a damper drive and attempt backwards time travel. My one and only goal was to find you and kill you in the most expedient way possible...and you, as well, Mr. Simonds. It was nothing personal toward you, just that you would be a target, too, if I were to find the two of you together. And I assumed I would.

"In my anger, I was hasty. I had not the patience for small time jumps. Of course I took a few tenuous steps backwards in time just to ensure I had the configuration correct. I did, where I was capable by myself. I had my own personal launch, which I had retrofitted with a jump drive so that I could accomplish this all without the need of any help.

"Of course, I knew from reading your book that once I arrived back in the 21st century, I would be marooned there permanently. That was a small price to pay for your death, Sandborn. I eagerly embraced it, such was my fury.

"But there was a practical consideration. I assumed I could get away with murder, given that I knew where you were and how to get you. Your body would have been forever hidden in Hornsey Wood Reservoir, and I would have been free.

However, I needed to have a means of survival here, so I decided to treat this as a sort of retirement. Why not? I was planning on retiring, anyway. Earth in the 21st century was probably as good as Earth in the 24th century, perhaps in some ways better as I had some idea of what the major historical events are for the next couple of decades, and I could prepare for and even thrive with that advanced knowledge.

"So I converted all my holdings to palladium, several tons of it. Palladium is relatively inexpensive in the 24th century, as its use largely disappeared with the extinction of the internal combustion engine. But here in the 21st century it is actually worth more than gold or even platinum. In fact, I quintupled my net worth by traveling back in time!

"I shuttled load after load of palladium to my launch and stuffed it into every hold, nook, and cranny. I used vacuum spaces between the inner and outer bulkheads. I piled it in every passageway until you could only get through sideways, if at all. In space, weight is irrelevant, so I filled my launch to overflowing.

"The increase in the launch's mass was substantial, and I did not take that into account in my calculations. As a result of taking bigger bites of time with increased mass, I overshot my mark and arrived here many months early."

"Ahriman, I suppose this is all very interesting, really, but is there a point here?" I had grown weary of his "lecture" and my sarcasm got the better of me.

"Patience, Sandborn, patience. I am getting to the point. When I arrived and realized how early I was, I made my priority, the setting up and funding of what would be a huge and extensive retirement account. I was able to sell a small amount of palladium to…I think they call it…a 'junk yard.' I sold enough at a couple of yards in various cities in the United States to gain some operating capital in US dollars.

Once I had that, I went to Switzerland and was able to spread enough around to attract the attention of some, um, investment brokers with enough of a moral deficit to act as a go-between and locate sources into which I could unload my cargo. And, of course, the broker was more than willing to set up a Swiss bank account into which I could deposit the proceeds...using multiple shell corporations, aliases, etc.

"It took some time, but eventually the deed was done. I am today one of the wealthiest men in the world that you've never heard of."

I was running out of patience. "So what?" I said. My petulance surprised me, but I was tired of his self-absorption.

"Because in turning that palladium into liquid assets, I got a firsthand look at how extremely greedy the people in this era are. I have never seen such avarice. I had thought the people of our own time were masters of the art of accumulation, but we are nothing compared to these people.

"And then it hit me. How easy it would be to manipulate these people into doing exactly what you wanted them to do if they thought there was profit in it for them. But my thoughts went no further. It was a mere curiosity, no more.

"As I settled in to wait for you to arrive at this time, I had little to do to pass the hours. So I picked up your book again, and this time read it in earnest. The first time I had been in a fury and I was scanning it for news of you and how to find you. This time, I read it carefully, absorbing the story. Before I had skimmed over the story of the chair and the experiences associated with it. I had skipped the descriptions of your changed life and the way it affected those around you. This time I considered the chair, the death experience, the life of service, and the dedication to helping others.

"And then my second epiphany happened. You were right. It is a new way, and a profound change from all I knew. It was a breakthrough in something that no one was looking for a breakthrough. I could have slapped myself for not seeing it before, but the way you both laid it out in the story made it unavoidable and undeniable."

Skip looked at me and I looked back. Could it be that Ahriman had experienced an awakening simply by reading the book? If so, it meant that the book exceeded even our wildest dreams. Change was possible apart from the chair.

"Yes. Go on," I coaxed.

"My dear Sandborn, I should not have to tell you of all people what happened or what I realized. You and your experience were the catalyst for my own understanding. I am forever a changed man. I see the total power of what you've been living and demonstrating by your life. You have found the secret of bringing people together to a common goal. You have found the secret to true success in any venture. By helping others, they help you, and as a result you achieve beyond what you could have achieved on your own. It is brilliant.

"All these years I have been relentless in my dominance of those around me and beneath me. I have exerted effort after effort to climb the ladder of success, to beat out my competitors, to amass holdings that give me power and prestige, to gain more power and prestige. I have been ruthless in my pursuit of success. I have ruined people who stood in my way. I have taken from people who were too naïve to stop me. I have subscribed to the simple Darwinian concept of the survival of the fittest.

"And it has worked for me. I have beaten out or beaten back anyone who stood in the way of my upward growth in influence and possessions. I have traded being ruled for ruling. In fact, I dare say I am an example of the pinnacle of achievement in my world.

"But there was never any rest, never any satisfaction. Yes, I ascended to the pinnacle, but I can never rest because there are always those who would seek to tear me down, to steal from me, to assert themselves over me. The drain, the pressure, the effort is constant. As I fought to get where I am, I fight to stay where I am.

"Your book, Sandborn. Your book showed me a better way. It was so simple I should have seen it all along. It is the next logical step. It is the evolution of competition to the next level. It is brilliant, but I repeat myself.

"Why fight, strive, and wrestle with those beneath you? Why expend your efforts to keep them down while you ascend? Why steal what you want when you can have it given to you? It is so plain, so simple, so logical. I should have seen it. But we are so smart and smug and self assured, of course we missed it. It took someone ideal like you, Sandborn, to show us the secret.

"Instead of making enemies, make friends. Instead of putting people down, lift them up. A rising tide lifts all boats. As you help others, it creates in them a sense of obligation for them to help you. But the numbers work for you. It is like a giant pyramid or Ponzi scheme. You divide yourself and help multitudes, and the multitudes focus on helping you.

"You help lots of people a little, and suddenly lots of people are helping you, contributing to you a lot. They are not afraid of you. They love you. They give to you. They enrich you. And they don't even realize they are doing it, because they see it as the natural response to the help they think you are giving them.

"The elite of us should have seen it. Oppression by kindness. Manipulation by sharing. Enrichment by humility. Only the masses don't see it as oppression, manipulation, or enrichment. They see it as generosity, as a spirit of community, as even ideal family.

"And yet, the result of your way and my way are the same. We are at the top of the heap with the most. We are the winners. We are the rich, the privileged, the elite. It's just with your way, you are secure. With my old way, I am constantly fighting and never secure.

"Your way is the inevitable Darwinian evolution of my way…it is my way only better."

"Now hold on, Ahriman. I don't think you've quite got it right," I said. "This has nothing to do with yourself. This has to do with others. This is not to advance your agenda. It is to enable growth in others."

"Of course, son. Of course it is. But that is only where it starts, my boy. What you haven't seen yet is that the fully realized truth is that as the originator and leader of this way of life, it will inevitably accrue to your benefit. People will owe their success to you, they will be beholden to you, they will bring their wealth to you. Dare I say it? They will worship you."

"No, no, no!" This time it was Skip. "I don't know this yet as well as Deke, but you've got this all wrong. This is never about you, and to be thought a god and worshipped is a total perversion of what Deke is about."

"There, there, Mr. Simonds. Why do people fail to see the potential of the truth that is revealed to them? This is as good as any religion, better in fact, because it enables adherents to worship a god they can see, not some invisible, unattainable entity."

Skip countered. "This is not about evolution, Ahriman. This is not the progression of a philosophy to some higher plane. This is entirely different. This is a transformation of a person. It is the reversal of their life. And this transformation as I understand it from Deke does not take you to the pinnacle. It takes you to the depths. You are not destined to be first by this life. You are destined to be last. You are not destined to be rich. You are destined to be satisfied."

"Rubbish. Defeatist trash. That is the pablum that religion

and philosophy have fed us for millennia. It is false humility. It is a sop that is offered to make the weak and ineffectual feel better. Men, real men, are genetically designed to fight and survive and win. They are physical and social carnivores, and they will never be happy any other way. Has not evolution taught us this simple truth: that pinnacle species survive and thrive through feeding on all other species? Why are you so shortsighted?"

"Because," I interrupted. "Because the essence of true maturity, true growth, true value is selflessness. Selfishness is the death of growth and goodness. Skip is right, profoundly and deeply right. It is not about evolution. It is about transformation. The chair itself was created to give us a transformative experience. It was never designed to make us a better version of ourselves. It was always intended to make us a totally different version of ourselves."

Ahriman looked shocked. He straightened himself in the chair and looked from me to Skip, back to me again.

"You cannot be serious. I assumed you were using the idea of the chair as a plot device, as an allegory for the growth in understanding you achieved. But you are convinced this chair is actually an agency of change, that you are somehow qualitatively different than you were before the chair. You have truly fooled yourselves into believing the fantasy you have created.

"Of course you cannot see the truth I am telling you because you are wedded to your own superstitious and fantastical concept of growth.

"I see I have given you too much, too quickly. I had not thought it possible that I could have developed this concept in my own mind in such a short time so much further than you in the years you've had it to yourself. But it is OK. I'm not offended. You'll no doubt consider what I'm saying and see the truth of it. After all, Deke, your freight business was the most successful and the most profitable of any independent. And I had data on all the independents in every district at my disposal. Your little enterprise was a profit-making machine. To my knowledge, certainly in my personal experience, there has never been a more successful venture. Even the merchant marine wasn't as profitable. We were just bigger.

"You just haven't realized how successful you were because you lacked the ability to carry your revelation to its logical conclusion. I have. What one could make by your method makes what I have amassed by mine look puny in comparison."

"Ahriman, you are either mad or deliberately ignorant. You cannot believe that all that the chair has taught was simply a better 'method' for getting rich. It is ludicrous. It is madness." I was shaking my head in disbelief.

"Why must you think so small and so backward, Deke? You know I'm right, surely somewhere deep within you, you realize that. Where civilization has missed the boat was trying to amass personal wealth through the oppression of others. You have discovered a far better way: the amassing of wealth voluntarily forfeited to you from those devoted to you. As they believe you are making their lives better, they give you far more than you could ever have gained by oppressing them. And they do it willingly."

"No," I said. "I reject everything you are saying. It is a monumental perversion of something that is wholly good, wholly noble, and wholly selfless. I could never follow this."

Ahriman raised his eyebrows. "You're serious, aren't you?"

"Deadly serious," I replied.

Ahriman hesitated, as though making up his mind. "I had come here today to offer you my help and my considerable resources to further the development of your philosophy. I believe I hold the key to your ultimate success and I am offering it to you, without strings or contingencies. Are you refusing this offer, really?" He spoke as though no sane man would possibly turn him down.

"Absolutely!"

"I will not offer it again, Sandborn. Consider your next words very carefully. I am a powerful friend to have. I am an even more powerful enemy."

"Then so be it, " I said. "I cannot trade the value of a life enabling others to be all they can be for a life that merely enables me to become rich. I utterly reject the idea of self-aggrandizement. If rejecting it means you are my enemy, that is not something I desire or choose. That is your choice, and it is on your head. I would live in peace with you, but it appears you will not allow it."

I was totally aware that I was making a fateful and irrevocable choice. I was aware it was not a small or inconsequential choice. And yet I could make no other.

"You are a small, shortsighted person, Deke. I could have made you powerful and enabled you to reach untold multitudes with your message. You could have effected a change in the here and now, not in the by and by. What you sought, I put within your reach, yet you refused to have the courage to grasp it. You are doomed by your own lack of imagination. You are doomed to live life on the margins, to only touch the few and ungrateful, and to die utterly alone. I pity you."

Ahriman stood, put on his coat, and headed for the door. He put his hand upon the knob, but hesitated. He did not turn back, but he spoke as to the door.

"You would have been my heir. Your greatness would have exceeded Deegan's and even my own. I would have made you my son."

And then he left.

CHAPTER 24 - **Epilogue**

Dear Reader,

It would be good, I suppose, if this book had a happy ending. It does not, but then neither is it an unhappy one. It just sort of ends, because that's what happens in real life. There is no "lives happily ever after" because there is a day after the moment you say that. And a day after that. And a day after that. It is the nature of life to just go on and on, oblivious of our desire, or even need, for a happy ending.

Ahriman left.

Deke and I wrote the rest of the story.

I used some of my retirement money to charter a plane to fly Deke, Bowie, and Angie to the United States. We avoided the authorities because it was a small plane and we landed in a small northern Maine private airfield. They got a social security card and a driver's license. They were ridiculously easy to obtain. We have yet to solve the citizenship thing, but it doesn't seem to matter as long as they want to stay in the US.

As of this writing, we have never seen Ahriman in person

again, although we are ever aware of his attention on and animosity toward us. Deke and I have embarked on writing a series of books, and Deke has gotten co-author credit on all of them. It has given rise to a host of public speaking opportunities for him, and he has developed a small but loyal following. We can tell it rankles Ahriman, because at every turn, he attempts to shut Deke up or down.

Ahriman does his work through intermediaries. He has a stable of lackeys that he has "bought" who do his dirty work for him. Most are functionaries in the media or publishing. Some are in law enforcement, and not a few in various elected and appointed government positions. He even owns a US senator or two. And he owns a best-selling author.

It is likely that Ahriman would just like to ignore Deke, but I suspect just Deke's mere existence is a nettle to Ahriman's ego and pride. More than once, he has taken it upon himself to counter successes that Deke experiences. If Deke has a successful seminar, one of Ahriman's public personalities will deride its success in the media. For every book Deke has written, Ahriman has published two or three promoting his own 'self-help' philosophy that takes the fundament idea Deke is putting forth but changes it enough to make it a get rich quick scheme.

Deke has told me on more than one occasion it would be fine if he could just "retire" in the sense of not being a public figure, and just live a quiet life in northern New England working at his trade (which is welding and metal fabrication, by the way). However, the more he seeks to be quietly assimilated into the local community, the more people get to know him and see his philosophy at work. And the more that happens, the more people begin to associate with him to learn and practice his way of life.

His "way of life" is just that: it is a way of "life." When others see him practicing the healthiness of helping and serving, they begin to see the lack of life in their own "way." So his reputation has grown from local to regional and threatens to grow further.

Perhaps that is what irritates Ahriman so much. Deke's impact is insurgent...he affects and influences people from the bottom up. His influence is personal and by example and local. Ahriman's is impersonal, by precept, not by example, and is international. He influences people from the top down. Where Deke simply lives his life in full view of others, Ahriman sets himself up as an authority of the "do as I say" type.

Ahriman (under a pseudonym) has become one of the most influential motivational speakers in the world. He may have been unknown in the 21st century that day he walked into my hotel room, but when he walked out, he started to promote what he calls "Help Yourself". What it amounts to, at least from our point of view, is a giant voluntary pyramid scheme that promotes selflessness among adherents by encouraging them to support Ahriman and recruiting adherents beneath them who are trained to support them. They believe the more money they send him, the more they will get themselves.

Ahriman gives them ideas and encouragement and even gifts and loans to prime the pump, but always to the end that some portion of it comes back to him. And he has whipped up a religious fervor among his followers. They would never think to criticize him.

Several of you have written to me (Skip) and pointed out what you consider holes in the story and/or problems with the science of it all. I am always grateful for any critique, be it good or bad, as long as it is well intended. And that which you have sent me has been more than respectful and polite.

Let me deal with the problem of paradoxes. Many of you

have pointed out that based on certain theories of time and space that if backward time travel were even possible (and you are convinced it is not) one could not change the past in any meaningful way. The "kill your grandfather" hypothesis is often given as a "proof". The paradox for those of you who don't know it is that if you went into the past intending to kill your grandfather, you might travel to that time, but it would be impossible for you to kill your grandfather because then, you would not be born. And if you were not born, you could not have traveled into the past to kill your grandfather. It is a true paradox. The assumption is that either you would find yourself somehow blocked from killing him (some sort of autonomic response, I suppose) or you could attempt to kill him, but he would always recover, regardless of the method you used. Or the guy you thought was your granddad wasn't really…he was a step granddad. Or. Or. Or.

The problem with this critique is that it starts from the assumption that the past is immutable. When you start with that as your basic assumption, you will always find "facts" to justify it. If you assume someone is a burglar, his actions will always be suspect and ultimately you will find "proof" he really is.

Let me be quick to say, some time is fixed. In fairness, there are points in history where the connection between the antecedent and the consequent is very, very taut. The more central an antecedent and its consequent are to the historical timeline, the more intractable they are. So there is an element of truth to the "Grandfather Paradox" in some cases at some points in time.

But Fi was right. Not all time is fixed. There are vast fields of mutable time, time which can be manipulated and changed with changed consequences, but with no ramifications that would ultimately rip the timeline apart. Such was my meeting with Deke in Victoria Station.

A few of you have brought up what you thought was an inconsistency in Ahriman's appearance at my hotel room. He said he had read the book, but the book clearly shows that his visit had absolutely no effect on Deke in convincing him to join Ahriman. If Ahriman had read the book as I said he did, Ahriman would not have bothered to even come to my hotel room.

There are two possible explanations.

The first is merely logical and rational. Ahriman read the book, knew it was pointless, but was so ego driven and with such a super inflated sense of self importance that he felt he could literally ignore history and change it. No one, in his mind, could resist him; such was his delusion.

However, the fact is he did read the book, and those chapters were just not there in the version he read. Let me explain.

We have always assumed that time unfolds in such a way that a completed act in the past has an impact on some reality in the future. I write a book in year X and it is then available to be read in year X + 100. And on some very simple level, that is true. A completed book in the present is available to be read as a completed book in the future.

But a book takes time to write. There is a time when it is an idea. There is a time when it is an outline. There is a time when it is only a couple of chapters long. In short, at any given time during the writing of that book, it exists only in some fragment of the finished book. That is obviously true.

What we haven't understood about the effect of changes in the timeline is that if the original change in the timeline is incremental, then the effect of those changes in the future is incremental, too. There are points where only the idea of the book exists into the future, or where only the outline, or only the first few chapters exist in the future. Why? Because we are free agents. Time does not decide that because we start a book, we are therefore going to finish a book. There are an infinite number of points along the timeline between where we decided to write the book and actually finish the book. As the author reaches each of those points, only that which he or she has finished up to that point can exist in the future... because at that moment, that's all there is.

The bottom line is that if the time between intending to write a book and finishing a book is six months, there is at any and every future point along the timeline from that moment on a six months development of that final book. If Ahriman picked a copy of my book up in the future while I was still writing it in the present, he would only get a copy that was as complete as where I was at that moment.

In all cases, since I completed the book, even if he had picked it up as incomplete, as I completed it in the present, it would have completed in the future. And once it completed in my present and the future, it would be to him as though it had always been completed.

But in Ahriman's case, he took the book and brought it back in time. By traveling backwards in time, he stepped outside the timeline, and for his copy of the book, it froze in whatever stage of development it was at that moment. And as ironic as it seems, the last chapters hadn't been written yet. He had no way of knowing what the outcome of that meeting was going to be.

Lastly, some of you have asked what became of Bowie and Angie. As I said, they came to the U.S. with Deke and me. Initially, the three stayed together until they had sufficient identification and had developed some idea of what they wanted to do in terms of work or a trade. All three moved away, but are still in regular contact with me. We meet together periodically, sometimes virtually, sometimes in real life. The three of them realize they are here for a purpose and are eager to pursue it.

But those are other stories for other times.

Lightning Source UK Ltd.
Milton Keynes UK
UKHW022221140421
381996UK00010B/2461

9 781087 946146